Murder Comes To U3A

Rob Elliott

PRINT ISBN: 978-0-473-47972-5

Fiction: thriller, serial killer, UK crime

Other titles by the author

Don't Come Back – a memoir and a love story about a Japanese woman from a famous family who sets off to start a new life in a foreign land.
[Reiko & Rob Elliott]

Have I Got a Deal For You – comic tales from the motor industry.

Behind the Mirrored Glass – the sequel, more comic tales from the motor industry

The Patient Pensioner – fraud on an international scale.

Short Stories for Short Trips

How to Survive Hip Replacement and Throw Away Your Walking Stick

The Pig Pesterer – a drug gang holds a woman hostage in a remote South Pacific location.

Dedication

I am deeply grateful to Sabine, Ryo and Kyoko and James and Rachel for the ongoing love, encouragement and support that I have received during the writing of this book.

Murder Comes To U3A

Rob Elliott

Chapter One

The spring of 2014 in England was a remarkable three degrees warmer than the spring of the previous year. The heavy rains which had marked the earlier months had now abated. The inhabitants of the small market town of Kings, north of London, were looking forward to a bright summer. Sadly, the state of the weather would become the least of their concerns as the year progressed.

Maria Luzzo had been playing bingo at the local hall for as long as anyone could remember. Every second Thursday was her night out. The regulars liked her sense of humour, and she was famous for the endless variety of silk scarves she wore.

Her husband Alan was a second-generation Italian. His father Adolpho had emigrated from Sicily after World War II. Maria and Alan had been married for more than forty years, and had raised three children; Mary, Christopher, and Lisa.

Alan's lifelong interest was in amateur theatre, both as an actor and a director. On his retirement from the bank he had been encouraged by a friend to join the local chapter of an international organisation called U3A: The University of the Third Age. Their credo immediately appealed to Alan as it was described to him as 'promoting lifelong learning'. Their members met monthly, but under the general umbrella of the parent organisation there were more than thirty special interest groups who studied a wide variety of topics from philosophy to art appreciation, money matters, jazz, and opera. The members of these groups met once or twice a month either in each other's homes, or if the interest was wider, in a suitable venue.

To Alan's delight, he found that there was a drama group, so he applied for general membership of Kings U3A, named for the district in which it was situated. He was soon accepted. Membership of the drama group quickly followed.

He had been going to the drama group meetings for about a year. During this period, the fourteen members of the group had discussed items from the world of the theatre: authors, plays, actors, music, and many other associated topics. At the February meeting, one of the lady members suggested that they should think about 'putting on a little show'. The membership of the drama group consisted of ten women and four men. This disparity was repeated right across the total membership of U3A. When the topic was raised, usually by newcomers, the comic in the group, Ron Barber, would answer, "it's because all the good men are dead, dear. All that's left is us poor miserable sods." This explanation usually closed down the conversation.

It was decided that a sub-committee would be formed to come up with suggestions for the March meeting. When the convenor asked for volunteers, Alan put his hand up first. He was joined by four ladies who were also keen to contribute. After more discussion, it was agreed that a play suitable for actors 'of a certain age' be found. "One with a little humour," suggested one of the ladies. "All everyone seems to talk about these days are their ailments."

At the March meeting, it was decided they would produce a two-act play by a well-known local playwright. It involved a cast of five – three women and two men. The scenario was in a café, and involved a married couple, a single woman, a widow, and a gay man.

Because of Alan's past experience he was chosen to hold auditions for the actors, and direct the production. He would co-opt members of the sub-committee to assist in other matters as required.

No sooner did the news get out than Alan was deluged with applications from hopefuls in the general membership who wanted to participate. They were to be disappointed, because the drama group had already decided to keep the play 'in house'.

Alan held the auditions and chose the cast with the target of presenting the play in August. Everybody was happy, except Mrs Lynda Osborne, who, as she pointed out to all and sundry, had been in several movies as a young woman, and her experience demanded that she be given a role, despite the fact that she was not a member of the drama group.

When she confronted Alan with her demands, he politely but firmly stated that the decision of the drama group to use only members of the group still stood.

"Very well then, Mr Luzzo, I shall join the drama group immediately."

"I'm terribly sorry Mrs Osborne, but I understand from the convenor that we are full, and in fact have a waiting list. If you put your name down now, you may be able to get membership, and try again next year, if we have another production."

"That's just not fair! I am the most qualified person in U3A."

"Rules are rules Mrs Osborne, I'm sorry."

"Well, we will just see about that Luzzo," she said, as she stormed off.

Rehearsals began, and they made good progress. Bill Chambers was chosen to play the role of the gay man. When one of the women in the cast suggested that he would have to make his voice sound 'more gay', he responded in an even deeper voice, saying that at least one of the All Black rugby team was gay.

Each Thursday night that Maria Luzzo went to play bingo, Alan would busy himself tidying up the kitchen, and then retire to their sunroom to watch re-plays of his favourite international golf tournaments on the Golf Channel. Maria would usually be home about nine-thirty, and he would have tea and biscuits ready so that he could catch up with the latest gossip from the bingo hall. The fact that now only two weeks were left before the U3A drama group play was to take to the stage, was uppermost in his mind.

Maria had insisted that she wasn't going to miss this Thursday night out because of a little rain. It was now mid-winter, and the wind was disturbing the branches on the trees growing close to the house. The leaves made a slapping sound against the windows, and the rain sent irregular streams of water cascading down the glass. He didn't worry about Maria, because their Honda was very reliable, and if the truth be known, she was by far the better driver.

Alan heard the faint ring of the front door bell. As he walked to the door at the end of the hall, he remembered Maria's warnings not to walk quickly or even worse, run to answer either the door or the phone. "You can't afford a fall," she would say, "you'll break your hip. It happens all the time to people of our age."

He opened the door, wondering who would be out in the rain on such a rotten night.

The security lights were on, but their coverage was dimmed by the rain. They revealed an average height person, wearing dark trousers and a rain jacket. He had a black woollen beanie on his head and a light scarf draped around his chin.

"Hello," said Alan, peering through the murk at the stranger, whose face was now in shadow. "What can I do for you?"

"Nothing," came the quiet reply.

Without warning, the stranger stepped forward, and grabbing Alan by the shoulders, pulled him off balance, at the same time slipping his hands up around Alan's neck.

Chapter Two

Maria carefully drove home, and was relieved when the automatic garage door lifted and the interior light came on. She had plenty to talk about with Alan. She locked the car and closed the garage door before letting herself out the side door and onto the short path to the front door steps.

At her second stride the security lights flashed on, revealing a dark shape lying on the path at the bottom of the steps.

She instantly recognised her husband's favourite blue sweater. It was now becoming stained dark red, as blood from a deep gash on her husband's head mixed with the rain to form a small puddle.

Her scream was silent at first, but quickly turned to a series of tortured shrieks, which the neighbours heard above the wind.

Seven minutes later, two policemen responding to the 111 call walked into a pathetic scene. A man and a woman were squatting beside Maria as she sat on the first step holding Alan's hand, while sobbing uncontrollably.

One of the policemen felt for a pulse. There was none.

A siren announced the arrival of an ambulance, and soon two medics joined the little group as the neighbours guided Maria out of the rain and up the steps to the shelter of her porch.

"Bad fall eh, mate?" said the senior policeman.

"Yes," said the medic, "but I would say that he was dead before he fell. Look at the angle of his neck. In my experience a fall down a few steps is not going to put anyone's neck at forty-five degrees. I will have to report this as a suspicious death."

The policeman didn't hesitate. He spoke into the microphone on his shoulder.

"Base 2, Base 2, car 27. We have a suspicious death, 1467 Grove Road, Kings. Repeat suspicious death at…"

"Base 2 to car 27. I got it the first time. Stand by. I will alert the serious incident squad. Secure and seal the area until they arrive."

The policemen donned extra wet weather gear from their car and began taping off the scene as the medics helped Maria.

Thirty minutes later, senior detective Guy Clapham and a police doctor arrived. Clapham had more than twenty years' service and was known as a meticulous investigator.

It took them only a few minutes to deduce that they could be dealing with a murder.

This was confirmed later the following morning, when the police forensic pathologist reported finding bruising around Alan's neck. There were no DNA traces, which indicated that the murderer was probably wearing gloves. The consensus was that murderer had expertly broken his victim's neck, and then thrown him down the steps. That indicated to Detective Clapham that they were looking for someone with either martial arts skills, or perhaps unarmed combat training in the forces. But later, as he pored over Mrs Luzzo's statement, he wondered just what motive anyone would have for killing a retired banker, who was currently occupied in producing an amateur theatrical.

Chapter Three

Mrs Lynda Osborne had survived a difficult marriage. She had met Roger Osborne when she had worked as a stripper at his club, while she was waiting for a movie audition. In her spare time she regularly went to a local gym to exercise with a women's dance group, so as to keep in trim for when the call came for her. Her agent always claimed this was, "just around the corner, luv." When it came, it turned out to be for a role in soft porn. After two or three short films, in which she appeared in the nude with no spoken lines, she decided to devote herself to selling cosmetics in an upmarket store. For this she developed an upmarket accent.

It was only after two years of marriage that she discovered that her husband was a 'fence'. He disposed of stolen property using his club to give the place an air of legitimacy, even if somewhat dubious.

A short time later, Roger served his first prison term of two years for handling a large amount of gold stolen from a pawn shop. His club was sold, and Lynda was left living in a small apartment. She had given up on the dance group, but still enjoyed going to the gym, where she had enrolled in an aerobics group. When Roger was paroled, Lynda supported them both. Nine months later, Roger was back inside, this time sentenced to serve ten years for armed robbery.

Eventually Lynda divorced him, and four years later married an older gentleman whom she had met while serving at the perfume counter in her store. He had been buying perfume as a gift for his wife, who was hospitalised at the time. A few months later he had appeared at the counter again, saying that his wife had passed away, and would Lynda like to have dinner with him sometime?

After four months, Lynda moved in with Ralph Sinclair, who was nineteen years her senior. She kept her job at the cosmetic counter, and Ralph, who was a retired engineer, spent most of his time either in the garden of his bungalow or at his golf club. They never discussed money, other than housekeeping, but she found him to be generous, and they had made two overseas trips together.

They had been living happily together for more than seven years, when disaster struck. Ralph was diagnosed with acute myeloid leukaemia, a disease which restricts the production of normal blood cells, leading to anaemia, and other symptoms. There was no cure available, other than a bone marrow transplant, and a donor for Ralph could not be found. After a year of weekly blood transfusions, he passed away.

Lynda was distraught. He had left her the house, and a small amount of investments, but the house was lonely without him. She loved the place, and the way that she had, with Ralph's encouragement, updated the furniture and had a new kitchen installed. She decided to stay in the house at least for a year or two.

But seven months later, Lynda was summoned to the office of the human resources manager to be told that the store was downsizing, and that her position was to become redundant. She would be given a redundancy payment based on her years of service, plus the accumulated savings in the company's pension fund, including the company contribution. The total sum was seventy-six thousand pounds. If she accepted the settlement as a retirement allowance, then it would be tax free.

Lynda accepted on the spot.

The idea of having a boarder in her house to supplement her income was suggested to her by a member of her U3A study group, which met every second Tuesday in the month to study modern art, a topic which had been a mystery to her. She had joined the local U3A chapter shortly after her retirement, and had become an enthusiastic contributor to its activities.

The first advertisement in the local newspaper produced four or five respondents, but none met her stipulation as to age, occupation, anticipated length of stay, and other interests. She had decided that if she was to share her table with anyone, she was entitled to know more than a little about them. The advertisement during the second week finally produced a candidate who seemed to meet Lynda's criteria, so she invited him to her home for a chat.

Her doorbell rang at exactly seven fifteen, the time agreed. She opened the door to find a rather slightly built man, immaculately dressed, smiling at her.

"Good evening Mrs Osborne, I am Thomas Tomlinson, here about the room?"

"Of course Mr Tomlinson, please do come in."

Lynda led the way into her lounge.

Over the following thirty minutes, Lynda learnt that he was an ex-naval officer, now employed as a marine claims adjuster for a major insurance company. She thought that he was in his late fifties. Satisfied with the responses to her questions, she showed him the room on offer. It was a large double room with an en suite bathroom, and windows over the garden.

"It's just what I am looking for, Mrs Osborne. Facing north it must get the morning sun. How nice. I am a bit of a private person, and I would like to have an electronic lock installed on the door if you decide to let me have the room. Of course, I would pay to have it done."

Lynda had no objection, in fact she thought that it was quite a good idea, as she would have no responsibility for the man's belongings.

As Tomlinson had already accepted Lynda's rental charge, she held out her hand.

"I'm more than happy for you to have the room Mr Tomlinson. When would you like to move in?"

"Would Saturday morning suit you, Mrs Osborne? I will arrange for a locksmith to contact you, so you can be home when he comes. By the way, please call me Tommy, everybody does. Oh, and I forgot to give you my card," he said producing a silver card case from his jacket pocket.

"That's lovely Tommy. I will see you on Saturday morning."

As he left, Lynda could not believe her luck. The man was clean and polite, almost like a caricature of Hercule Poirot, the TV detective, but without the moustache.

Almost three months had passed since Tommy had moved in. He kept very much to himself, and Lynda had never seen him without a collar and tie, neatly pressed trousers, and highly polished shoes. She supposed that his naval training had imbued him with that discipline. Tommy had told Lynda that he belonged to an ex-naval officers' club called The Old Salts, and he enjoyed keeping up with a few old friends. He was away from time to time, as he explained that his job required travel, both domestic and international. Lynda had never been in his room since his arrival, as he insisted on doing his own cleaning. She left fresh linen on a chair outside his room every Friday, and assumed that he had his laundry done professionally, especially his shirts.

She was curious at the time about the large two-door steel cabinet that was delivered when he moved in, but soon forgot about it.

Chapter Four

On this Friday morning Tommy had got the morning paper from the box at the front gate, while Lynda prepared a simple breakfast. Tommy never asked for anything other than a boiled egg, toast and coffee.

As Lynda sat down, Tommy folded his paper.

"Mrs O," (she had not yet invited him to call her by her Christian name) "you mentioned that the U3A man who was rude to you was named Luzzo?"

"Yes, the horrible man, and his stupid play. Why?"

"Well I'm sorry to say, but he is dead. His wife found him on the steps outside their house last night, and the paper suggests that it might be murder."

Lynda clattered her tea cup down on the saucer.

"What! A U3A person murdered? It can't be, how awful. Was he shot or something?"

Tommy picked up the paper again.

"No, it says here that he somehow had a broken neck. Very strange."

"But who would want to kill him? I regret saying that he was horrible. It was just that we didn't see eye to eye. Maria, his poor wife, what will she do?"

"You said that he was a retired banker, Mrs O, so I expect that he would have life insurance," said Tommy matter-of-factly.

"I hate funerals, but I suppose I'll have to go," said Lynda. "All of U3A will be there."

"Now don't you go getting too upset Mrs O, I'm sure that she will be taken care of, you know family and all that."

"Yes. I suppose so. I know there are two daughters living in town. By the way, Tommy, how was your dinner at the club last night? I'm sorry, I forgot to ask."

"Very pleasant indeed Mrs O, but you must excuse me or I'll be late for the office."

"Of course Tommy, have a nice day."

Lynda sat quietly reading the article. What would happen to the play now, she thought? With no director surely it would have to be abandoned?

The morning after the funeral, Tommy asked Lynda about the gathering.

"It was so sad, and just as I thought, there were a huge number of our members there. In a way it must have been some comfort for poor Maria to know that she has so much support. Alan's son Chris gave a beautiful eloquent eulogy. He is such a lovely man. He brings in cars from Japan, and he sold me mine."

"How nice," said Tommy. He quickly corrected himself. "Sorry, Mrs O, I meant the car not the funeral, of course. There is no such thing as a nice funeral is there?"

With that, he retired to his room to get ready to leave for the office.

One week after the funeral, Mrs O got a call from Thelma Hope, a member of the drama group, saying that she had been asked to take over the production, and that had created a vacancy. Mrs Hope had heard that Lynda had acting experience, and would she like to help out in the crisis? It took only a moment for Lynda to agree. After all, she reflected, U3A was founded on voluntary community service. It would be rude of her not to accept the invitation.

When she told Tommy the news, he was philosophical.

" *So shines a good deed in a naughty world*', Mrs O," he said, quoting Shakespeare. Lynda was impressed. How original, she thought.

Chapter Five

Detective Clapham had been poring over the statements taken from Mrs Luzzo, her family and members of Alan's wider circle, including some members of U3A. There was nothing to suggest that he had any enemies anywhere. Even a check on his career in banking showed a man of high integrity regarded with general respect. Yet Clapham had to face the facts. An autopsy report from the pathologist had concluded that Alan Luzzo had been the victim of a very professional attack. He had been killed in a classic two-step martial arts move, where the victim is first pulled off balance, and then caught round the neck, so that in the one movement the victim's neck is swiftly twisted and broken. The distinct bruising around his neck gave evidence of a very strong grip. The attack would have been silent, and over in seconds.

Very neat, thought Clapham, no weapon needed.

The first policemen on the scene had noticed nothing unusual, and a careful examination of the murder area the following morning had revealed nothing significant in the way of evidence.

Both his senior inspector and the media were asking for a progress report. All he could venture was that his department were continuing with their inquiries.

He called a meeting of the team which had been assembled to carry out the Luzzo murder inquiry. Pointing to various aspects of the case which had been highlighted, he said, "Ok folks listen up. So far we have nothing. Now I want to examine the background of every member of this U3A outfit. It could be that one of these bloody golden oldies might have somehow, somewhere, had training in unarmed combat, and has had enough confidence to put it into effect."

"Guy, does that mean we should also look at the women?" The question came from Louise Banks, the youngest member of his team.

"Yes, Lou, as far as I can remember, girls were being admitted to karate classes as far back as the fifties and sixties. You never know, there may be an old black belt lurking under one of those blue rinses. Count nobody out until we get some sort of lead. There are over two hundred members, so divide them up amongst yourselves. The membership secretary has provided all their contact information. I want details of age, education, marital status, family members, health, careers, the works, including any previous. We need an active and complete database, and fast. And one more thing, listen to the gossip. My mother once told me that women of a certain age have one thing in common, they love to gossip. That's all, now get going!"

Chapter Six

It was Tim Cormack's turn to host the nine members of the U3A wine appreciation group, which held a monthly meeting in each of the member's homes by rotation. His wife had prepared a rather extravagant afternoon tea before she readied herself to go to her bridge afternoon.

"Tim, dear," she said, as she departed, " the last thing we need is for a few drunken old men to upset the evening traffic, so make sure everyone has something to eat."

Tim smiled as he placed half a dozen brown paper bags on the cabinet in the dining room where the discussion and tasting would take place. Each member contributed twenty pounds a month so the two members chosen to buy the wine for the next meeting would have enough cash to cover a wide spectrum of wine. Each bottle would be placed in a bag, so that the supposedly finely tuned palates of the members could make their determinations. Opinions would be given, guesses made, comparisons explained, and some pretentious descriptions offered.

Notes were kept in a large journal. Tim's favourite was the comment on a rather pungent Australian shiraz. "It showed hints of freshly trimmed hedgerows, damp earth and rotten leaves."

When the other eight members arrived, the meeting began with a short presentation by one of the members who had just visited the Bordeaux region. Ron Barber, the joker in the group, made a fake yawn, cupping his hand over his mouth. He still dabbled as an insurance agent claiming that 'old insurance agents were like old soldiers, they never died.' Bert Travers smiled and carried on.

"One of the highlights was a visit with the Demptos family," he said. "They have been providing the oak barrels for the premier crus for about a hundred and fifty years. They used to get their oak from Lebanon, but the civil war there put a stop to that. These days it comes from all over, they even have a plant in the Napa Valley. There is a trade in used barrels, so that the second grade growers can claim that their reds are matured in the same barrels as the world's best."

"Typical bloody French," commented Ron Barber.

Nobody laughed.

The meeting went on, and as the third bottle was examined, the conversation, as usual, got a little more raucous.

"Poor bloody old Alan Luzzo getting pushed down the steps of his own house. Not a nice way to go. The papers are saying that it is murder. More like jealous husband syndrome, I'd say," said one.

Tim Cormack chipped in, "That's a bit tough old man, why the hell would you think that?"

The man tapped the side of his nose. "One hears things, you know?"

"One hears woodpeckers too mate, but it doesn't mean that the whole bloody tree is going to fall down."

They all grinned. Ron Barber had struck again, and the topic went back to the wine.

During the interval for afternoon tea, Tim took aside the man who had commented on Alan's death.

"Do you really know something?" he asked.

"Not really," said the man. "The wife heard some gossip about his son Chris being caught up in a fraud involving the importation of some used cars from Japan. Alan had financed some of it, but half of the cars were on consignment and Chris sold them, keeping most of the money. The suppliers in Japan were pretty upset. For God's sake don't mention it, you know, *in vino veritas*."

Chapter Seven

Ten days had passed since the murder, and the team operating under Guy Clapham had interviewed almost half of the U3A members on the list. They were finding that in almost every instance, the person being interviewed had a theory about the case. These ranged from an attack by a man trying to get appointments for the demonstration of a new type of vacuum cleaner to an argument with a religious person or persons trying to deliver a doorstep sermon. While they were original, the theories were not enough to get Clapham excited.

Constable Louise Banks knocked on Clapham's open door.

"Well don't just stand there, tell me something, Lou."

"Sorry, but I have a question. Do you think that we should re-interview Mrs Luzzo? I just read her statement again, and it is pretty thin in the areas we are now covering with the U3A members. It was taken the morning after, when she was still traumatised."

"Why didn't I think of that?" replied her boss. "Alright then, get onto it, and let me know if you open any doors – or even any small cupboards, if it comes to that."

Constable Banks rang Mrs Luzzo, and asked if she could see her for a chat about some of the details in her original statement. She also suggested that it might be more comfortable for her to have a family member or friend present at the time. Mrs Luzzo agreed to meet her the following afternoon.

Louise noticed a light stain still visible on the path below the bottom step where Alan Luzzo had died. Mrs Luzzo invited her into her lounge and introduced her daughter Lisa, whom she had invited to be present.

"Thank you for seeing me, Mrs Luzzo. I know how difficult these days have been for you. I just want you to know we are committed to finding your husband's killer just as soon as we can. There may be some small, seemingly insignificant detail which will provide us with the lead we are seeking."

Lisa spoke. "Of course Constable Banks, we want to help, but we thought you had taken Mum's statement already."

"That's right, but we have widened the inquiry, and that involves asking one or two additional questions, if you don't mind?"

"I don't mind," said Mrs Luzzo, "ask away."

"Well it involves your family and friends' interests, including hobbies and travel. Have you or any of the family ever been to Japan?"

Lisa glanced at her mother. "Yes, I spent a term there on a student exchange some years ago. I still write to the family in Kamakura."

"Any other family members?"

Again Lisa looked her mother's way. There was a moment of silence.

"My son has been to Japan, and has had some business problems there. What has that to do with my husband's death?"

"It is probably irrelevant, Mrs Luzzo. Can you tell me the nature of the problem? It will remain absolutely confidential, I assure you."

"I don't know much, Alan was handling it, but we did have to give Christopher a lot of money to square up with the Japanese over some debt. Alan said it was not Chris's fault. It was something about insurance, but it was all settled about a year ago."

"Is he still in the business Mrs Luzzo?"

"Well yes, but he is working for someone now, so he has no actual financial involvement," said Maria.

After checking a few more details from Mrs Luzzo's original statement, Louise closed her notebook and stood up.

"Thank you Mrs Luzzo, and you too Lisa, we will report any progress to you as it occurs. In the meantime, please remember that we have counsellors available to support you anytime you or the family feel that you would like to talk about your bereavement."

Lisa saw her to the door.

"Constable, please catch the bastard!"

"We will Lisa, we will," said Louise.

Two hours later Detective Topham was reading Louise's notes.

"So it appears that the son had to be bailed out by his dad on some shonky car deal. Japanese involved. Louise, you might have opened a door."

She smiled. "So you think Alan Luzzo was topped by a teen-age ninja turtle?"

"Very clever," said Topham, "but maybe it was just an ordinary ninja. A kind of message to other dealers to behave. A lot of the used car trade in Japan is controlled by the Yakuza gangs. It is said that on an international basis they have vertically integrated the business. They own some of the auction houses in Japan where the cars are sold, then these are transported on special ships called car carriers. At the final destination the cars are distributed to local dealers. You can guess who owns the finance company and the insurance company. It must be a nice little earner! Gang members usually just kill each other, but I'm told that they make exceptions from time to time. I wouldn't rule it out. Louise, why don't you and the team check with immigration, and see if any single male Japanese tourist flew in and out of here in the days before and after the murder?"

"Maybe they got the wrong man, sir?"

"Good God Louise, don't be that devious. I'm having enough trouble sleeping as it is."

Chapter Eight

Early on in the establishment of Kings U3A, the committee had observed that with a preponderance of women members, many of whom had left financial matters to their late husbands, they needed some professional advice in handling their assets. So a new group was formed: Money Banking & Finance. It was an instant hit with both female and male members, so much so that more than forty members signed up. That meant that the usual policy of meeting in each others' homes would not work, and so a suitable hall was found at a peppercorn rental. A convenor was appointed, and also a small sub-committee formed to find suitable experienced speakers for the monthly meeting.

Mrs Jean Adams had immediately joined. When her husband had passed away she found that she was far more wealthy than she had realised. She enjoyed a small but not insignificant income from shares that she held in a company established by her late father, which had recently made an IPO.

When her lawyer had informed her that her husband had left her approximately four million pounds, her first question to him was, could she now buy a new car? Mr Adams had accumulated his wealth by not spending any money on items that he saw as utilities, like cars. While he was alive, he wrote all the cheques, paying all the bills. The lawyer suggested that Mrs Adams should consult a financial advisor.

The couple had no children, and she began to think about suitable charities, and education, as areas where she could help a little. As a retired teacher, she knew how many smaller schools struggled to provide much-needed support for their children, especially in the fast-moving area of IT.

She was delighted to read in the latest U3A newsletter that the speaker for the next meeting was to be a banker, who specialised in personal banking. She was not aware that all the big banks had a dedicated department for those customers whose activities were at such a level that it demanded they get special service and attention. The purchase of her new mid-size Mercedes Benz had introduced her to another special service. The nice young salesman at the dealership had even sold her old Saab for her.

Lynda Osborne was also planning to attend the same meeting, because as a member, she had learned so much about managing her own affairs. One secret investment she had kept from her failed first marriage was the black weight she used as a front door stop. It was a solid silver ingot. Her former husband had painted it black, and asked her to look after it while he was in prison, but he must have forgotten about it when he moved to Australia on his release. She assumed it was stolen, but had heard somewhere about a statute of limitations, and anyway, nobody had ever claimed it. With silver at about $US17 an ounce, she had a four thousand pound doorstop. Wouldn't Tommy be surprised if he knew, she smiled to herself.

That evening over dinner, Tommy told Lynda he was having two days off work to prepare for a short overseas trip on a business matter. She knew he was involved in insurance, but she never asked any questions. As the next meeting of the Money Banking and Finance Group was the following morning, on the spur of the moment she asked Tommy if he would like to accompany her as a guest. She explained the purpose of the meeting, and after a little thought he accepted the invitation.

"Thanks Mrs O, but I will have to be back by 1 p.m. to check my emails. I'll slip away towards the end of the meeting, if you don't mind?"

"No problem," she replied, "we can take two cars, and you can leave when you're ready. I'll explain how to get there."

Promptly at 10 a.m., the convenor opened the meeting and welcomed the more than forty members present. He also welcomed Mr Thomas Tomlinson, who was a guest of Mrs Lynda Osborne.

There was an immediate shuffling of chairs as heads bobbed back and forth trying to see who Mrs Osborne had invited. This kind of event was what made U3A so interesting in the minds of many of the members.

The expert on personal banking was introduced, and for the following forty-five minutes he gave a very professional Power-point presentation to his audience. As usual, at least three of them were asleep towards the end. It was time for a coffee break and a stretch as the members assembled in an ante-room.

In one of the little knots that formed as members enjoyed their coffee, Jean Adams joined Lynda and Tommy plus three other members, including Ron Barber.

With a hint of the confidence that her new financial position had brought her, Jean introduced herself to Tommy.

"And what business are you in Mr Tomlinson, assuming that you are too young to be retired?"

Tommy winced and coughed. "I'm in insurance," he replied, trying not to make too much eye contact.

"Oh, how very interesting. When Alf died, I had to review my insurance, especially the contents. One seems to accumulate so much these days, don't you think?"

"Yes," said Tommy, "and from my experience it is best to get accurate valuations, and keep up to date."

"I agree. Alf was crazy about stamps. I can't imagine why, I find the whole topic boring, but he said he had been a collector since he was a small boy. Anyway I got an expert in, and he said that it was among the best collections he had ever seen, worth many thousands. Dear Alf knew what he was doing after all."

"Yes," Ron Barber grinned. "As a hobby, stamps can't be licked."

Lynda interrupted. "Excuse us, I would like to introduce Tommy to the president over there."

She grabbed Tommy's elbow and steered him across the room."

"I'm sorry about that, Tommy. They say her husband left her ten million pounds when he died, and she has changed for the worse. And as for that Barber fellow, he is just stupid."

"It happens, Mrs O, it happens," was all he said.

The meeting continued, and there was time for a Q&A session towards the end.

Questions to the speaker covered a wide range, asking for tips for the share-market. Were enduring powers of attorney a good idea? Should one have a 'cash stash' in case ATMs crashed?

Tommy excused himself to Lynda and slipped out of the hall.

Chapter Nine

Louise Banks had met Barry Smart about six months after graduating from the police college and being assigned to the King's area police station. Barry was the general reporter and sub-editor of the small local newspaper, the *Kings Herald*, 'est:1897' as it proudly proclaimed on the masthead.

Despite the inroads of social media, the publishers, a group of local businessmen and councillors, managed to get out two copies a week with a circulation of seven thousand. Barry Smart had a diploma in journalism and had been employed by the paper for two years. He had been born in Kings and knew everyone, and everyone knew him as he passed by on his little motor-scooter accompanied by a cloud of blue smoke.

They had met at the local squash club, and it had been love at first sight. Louise loved Barry's enthusiasm for life. His dream was to break 'a really big story'. She felt sure that having had time to observe his methods, one day he would realise that dream. He listened to gossip, went to council meetings, visited shopkeepers, kept in touch with the local sports clubs – he was everywhere.

Louise soon found out that he had been to her police station asking questions about progress in the Luzzo murder case. Detective Clapham had forbidden her to pass on anything about the case. When she pointed this fact out to Barry, he was quick to respond.

"So you don't love me, eh?"

"Yes I do, you idiot, so don't try the old pillow talk trick, it won't work."

"We'll see." He smiled. "Anyway I'm counting on something coming out of the oldies at Kings U3A. It's a hotbed of gossip. I'll bet if there is anything going on, they'll be the first to know."

"Let's change the subject," she said in a rather husky voice, drawing back the duvet to reveal that she was naked.

Detective Clapham was becoming desperate. He had pored over the interviews and found nothing likely to lead to the identity of the killer. The forensic examination of the crime scene had turned up virtually nothing because the storm on the night of the murder had washed away any evidence. There were no identifiable footprints, and with no weapon being used it was almost the perfect murder. All that he was left with was a small plastic evidence bag containing what looked like the small folded paper cover usually attached to a sticking plaster. One of his team had noticed it under a leaf in the garden next to the steps where Alan Luzzo had been found. His first thought was that it had been blown in off the street during the storm, but he'd sent it to the national crime laboratory in the capital for analysis.

Some days later he got a call from the chief forensic scientist at the crime lab.

"Detective Clapham, we have had a good look at the piece of paper that you sent us. No fingerprints, but one of my team is a stamp collector and he was the one doing the analysis. He is 99% sure that it's part of a stamp collector's hinge. Let's call it the sticky bit you put on the back of a stamp, so you don't have to actually stick the stamp to a page in your album. The adhesive used is much milder than the one you get from sticking plaster. Could be you are looking for a stamp collector, Detective."

Clapham blinked. "Who the bloody hell collects stamps these days? It's all electronic messaging. But thanks anyway, and please pass on my thanks to your technician."

"Happy to help, I hope you get your man, sir."

Did this mean that they had to go back to every bloody U3A member and ask who amongst them was a stamp collector? The U3A president had already warned him that some of the older members were very upset at the thought that one of their members was a killer. Another round of questioning would test everyone's patience. He put his head in his hands, then called for a staff meeting at eight the next morning.

At eight-twenty his meeting was disturbed by a detective from the burglary squad.

"Sorry to interrupt your meeting Guy, could I have a brief word outside?"

Clapham followed the man into the corridor, closing the door behind him.

"Bad news I'm afraid, mate," he said. "We got a call about a burglary a few minutes ago so I sent a car there. They first found a distraught cleaning lady, and later, a woman's body in an upstairs bedroom. She was wearing a nightdress and had probably been killed during the night. The cleaning lady had called out 'anyone home?' when she entered the house, and saw some cabinets open. She was so confused when she called 111 that she didn't mention a body. We've set up a crime scene for you, and my staff are there now."

"Have you got a name?"

"Yes, she is Mrs Jean Adams, or was."

"I hope to God she wasn't a U3A member," he said, as he went back into his meeting to break the news.

When he asked his team if anyone could remember interviewing a Mrs Jean Adams from U3A, he got the wrong answer.

"I did boss. Nice lady," replied an acting detective.

"Well, I am afraid that she is a dead lady, and we have got a problem."

A hush went round the room as the news sank in. Two U3A members killed in two weeks.

At the house, the scene was calm. A female constable was looking after the cleaning lady. Clapham was waiting for the arrival of the forensic team from headquarters, together with a police doctor, when the chief inspector for the area arrived.

"The woman's body is upstairs sir, there is no sign of a weapon being used, and her nightwear is undisturbed, shall I say. Strange thing is that she is lying on the bed, not in it. We'll have some idea of the cause of death as soon as the doc gets here."

If Clapham felt that the inspector's thoughts were elsewhere, they were.

"What are we going to tell the press, Clapham? You have got no suspect in the Luzzo case, and now we have another death. Don't just stand there man, give me some answers."

"Sir, we may be looking for a stamp collector."

"You can't be serious."

"Well it is the only clue that we have at the moment, sir."

The police doctor arrived just in time to save Clapham, at least for the moment.

Five minutes later, he came down the stairs to where Clapham was waiting with his superior.

"I think your killer may have struck again gentlemen," he said, in the matter of fact way that some in his profession do. "The poor woman has been strangled. She may have put up a little resistance because there were residual scraps of skin under her fingernails.

"Not a single blow, you say?" asked the inspector.

"No sir, I would say there is evidence of a struggle. I'll have a full report ready by tomorrow morning, but I don't expect to have much to add, except an estimate of the time of death of course."

The inspector thanked the doctor and turned to Clapham.

"You're going to need extra staff Clapham, so I intend to second two more investigators from HQ to assist you. We'd better apprehend this brute before the whole town goes into panic mode. Now please explain your earlier reference to a stamp collector."

The detective detailed the contents of the forensic report.

As the inspector left, a member of the burglary squad came out of the lounge.

"Guy, we have completed the scene examination from our side. The cleaning lady can't identify anything missing, so apart from a few opened bureaus and cupboards, the place is clean. I think we can assume the killer was wearing gloves, and maybe found whatever it was he was looking for. I will contact her insurance company, when we find out who it is, and get a contents list so that we can have a more thorough determination."

"OK, and thanks. Keep on it, and start combing your files to see if you have any names with form who might be into martial arts."

Clapham quickly decided to call in a criminal profiler, and asked one of his staff members to contact HQ to see who they would like to nominate for the task. Next he called Morris Kincaid, the president of Kings U3A, to advise him of the death of Mrs Jean Adams, and to find out when the next general meeting of members was scheduled.

The man spluttered in disbelief. "What did you say? Jean Adams? Good God, what is going on? How did she die?"

Clapham decided to lie. "We are treating it as an unexplained death at the moment, sir, and we will have a report on the cause of death in a day or two. I know this news will shock your members, and I suggest that the chief inspector may want to address your next meeting to help to allay their fears. When is the next meeting?"

"The day after tomorrow. Bloody hell, wait till this hits the news, the media will have a field day. I can tell you, Detective what's-your-name, the only thing that will allay the fears of my members is for you to stop this bloody mayhem by catching the culprit, because I suspect right now, that this is another murder."

"Sir, keep calm, and my name is Clapham. Either I or a member of my staff will keep in touch with you. Feel free to call me at any time."

Clapham put down his phone. He had a headache.

Chapter Ten

At eleven a.m. Barry Smart was waiting in the reception area of the Kings Police Station for Louise to finish her shift, as he wanted to take her out to lunch before she went home to sleep for the afternoon. The duty sergeant appeared behind the counter.

"Gidday young Barry, don't hang around out here, you make the place look untidy."

Barry managed a smile. He had to keep on good terms with the sergeant because he was always asking him for news for his 'Out and About' column.

"Anyway, you're wasting your time if you're waiting for 'Shirley Holmes' because she's at an unexplained death scene over on One Mile Road."

"Shit, why didn't you tell me that first?"

"Didn't think you'd be interested."

Barry's scooter baulked three times before it fired. Entering One Mile Road, he soon spotted three police cars about two hundred yards ahead.

Standing his scooter on the grass, he ran up the path to the house, only to be stopped by a local constable standing behind the familiar yellow tape of a crime scene.

"Slow down you," yelled the policeman, "this is a no-go area, so stop right there."

"I'm with the press and I have questions to ask," said Barry, undaunted.

"There is nothing here for you to see, so why don't you just piss off and wait to see if there is an official announcement this afternoon."

"What time?"

"I have no bloody idea. It'll be when the boss decides. But with the mood he is in at the moment, I wouldn't plan on asking any questions."

"Why is he in a bad mood?"

"Because dummy, he has two unsolved murders on his hands."

"So this is a murder?"

"No it's an unexplained death."

"But you said two murders."

"I made a mistake. Now stop hassling me and go away or I'll have you for trespass."

Barry retreated. Outside the property, he rang his editor. The next publication date for the *Kings Herald* was tomorrow. He told the editor that he had some sensational news which he thought might warrant a special edition. His boss agreed to meet him at the office.

This time his scooter fired first time, which he took as a good omen.

Chapter Eleven

Clapham had just got back to his desk and welcomed the two detectives from HQ, when the phone rang. He was rehearsing what he was going to say to the inspector, but it was the police pathologist.

"Guy, I'm just about to write my report on this morning's victim, but I thought you would like to know the official verdict now."

"Thanks, Doc, so?"

"So the poor woman died as the result of strangulation, constricting the throat and cutting off the air supply. There was also a dislocation of several vertebrae, probably caused as her neck snapped back. Death would have been almost instantaneous. I'll email the report to you later. Any questions?"

"Can I assume there were no other injuries at all?"

"Nothing, so if you're thinking of a sexual motive, you are out of luck, I'm afraid."

"Thanks Doc. I hope I don't have to call on you again this year or next."

His phone rang again. It was the desk sergeant.

"Guy, could you come out front for a moment please? You're not going to like it."

Wearily, Clapham eased out of his chair, excused himself to his two new arrivals, and made his way to the reception area.

Instantly, he recognised the thug standing in the lobby. It was the local tow-truck driver. He had an endless number of minor convictions to his name. Everyone hated him.

"Gidday, Mike, come to give yourself up?" enquired Guy.

Mike Jones looked serious.

"Just doing the right thing, mate."

"That'll be a first. Get to the point."

"The bloody secretary at the golf club phoned me to tow a wreck that had been left burnt out overnight on the waste ground next to the driving range. So I take meself there, and as soon as I step out of the bloody truck, the dog goes bananas. There's a corpse in the front seat. The bloody fire must have gone out before it totalled the whole bloody car. The golf guy said he had only looked at it through binoculars from his office, lazy bastard. So I've come straight here. I haven't touched nothing."

"Wait here Mike, speak to nobody, while I get a squad together." He looked at the sergeant.

"Get on the blower and tell everyone in the investigative department to get in here now."

He hurried back to his office.

"You guys are going to be busy. We have another possible murder on our hands."

"What? You are talking about Jean Adams, right?"

"No, this one's in a burnt-out car. Let's go."

The two new arrivals looked at each other in blank amazement.

The scene at the golf club was almost out of hand when the police party arrived to take charge. Various employees of the golf club had gathered, as well as a knot of members who were standing off to one side.

Clapham took charge.

"All stand back please, at least ten yards. This is now a crime scene and we don't want the whole place contaminated by you all milling around. Now move!"

There was a general nodding of understanding as they all obeyed the instruction.

The police doctor, who Clapham had been speaking to only an hour or two before, arrived in a police Land Rover. He had not wanted to get stuck on a golf course, but fortunately the course was very dry and the police cars had not had any trouble.

"Here we are again Guy, we will have to stop meeting like this, people will talk."

"Well the poor bastard in the car is past talking, I would say."

As the doctor carried out an examination of the body while it was still in the car, an ambulance arrived. With the car screened, he could only determine that the body was that of a male.

"Any personal items visible, Doc?"

"Not at first glance Guy, better leave that to the forensic team, they are on their way."

Clapham glanced at the car again. The registration plates had been removed and the heat of the fire had shattered the front screen, destroying any stickers that might have provided a clue as to ownership.

"Well at least we know that it used to be a Honda," observed one of Guy's new team, pointing to a badge on a small rear part of the car that had survived. "If we can get a VIN number off the identification plate on the bulkhead, we might get lucky."

The arrival of a forensic investigator from HQ allowed for a closer examination of the corpse and the remains of the vehicle. With the aid of a short crowbar he was able to lever open the front bonnet. The plate with the VIN number was smoke blackened, but after he rubbed it with a small rag and a drop of petrol he was able to read out the number to an assistant who jotted it down in his notebook.

Clapham asked his squad member to call the Motor Vehicle Registration Office for an ID. The man stood away from the wreck and spoke on his cell-phone for nearly five minutes before returning to Clapham.

"Guy," he whispered, not wanting any of the onlookers to hear. "It is registered to a Christopher Luzzo."

Chapter Twelve

Mr Thomas Tomlinson settled back in his business class seat on Cathay Pacific flight CP 105 bound for Hong Kong. He reflected on how busy he had been these last few days, and that he really deserved a break. Hong Kong had gone through dramatic change over the years that he had been travelling there.

He missed the old days when as a passenger on British Airways he was occasionally invited into the cockpit on the approach to the old Kai Tak airport. On the mountain ridge he would see the huge illuminated arrow with its 'TURN RIGHT' instruction. At that moment the huge aircraft would bank and skim in over the tops of the buildings surrounding the airport, just above the washing lines. He'd found it equally exciting approaching from the harbour end, where the aircraft flew up a canyon of apartment buildings at very low altitude over the water, just before touching down.

This time, the huge Airbus thundered into the new airport, some distance by rail from the CBD.

Tommy was soon on the train into town. Although many new hotels had been built to accommodate the hordes of tourists now visiting from mainland China, he had always stayed at the Miramar Hotel on Nathan Road, and saw no reason to change. They knew him there, and he had a comfortable familiarity with all the lanes around the hotel. He would also take the opportunity to have his Rolex serviced at King Fook, the famous jeweller and watch retailer, a few steps away on Nathan Road. David's Shirt Shop just around the corner would have his six new shirts waiting. His measurements had not varied over time, and a simple email order was all that was required.

At Lane Crawford, he would spend some time in the men's department replacing the old clothing that he would leave at the hotel when he departed

As he ordered a BLT sandwich and a pot of tea from room service, he wondered how Mrs O was coping with all the trouble that was being visited on Kings U3A. Privacy was what he valued the most, and he had felt it unnecessary to reveal his real name to her. People were so nosey. She reminded him of his own mother – kind, respectful and caring, with old-fashioned good manners. He considered himself fortunate to have found her. Tomorrow he would go to Khan's Rug Emporium just across the road from the Hong Kong Central Police Station and buy her a new rug. He thought that the one that she had in the lounge has seen better days.

Travelling first class on the Star Ferry to the main island had always appealed to his sense of humour, but not as much as the free taxi ride he would get to Khan's. All one had to do for that was, on getting into the taxi, say in an authoritative voice, "Central Police, driver," whereupon the driver would straighten up in his seat, check all his mirrors and carefully set off, assuming that he had a policeman on board. At the entrance to the station Tommy would say, "this will do thank you, driver." The man would drive off in a hurry, refusing any payment. Tommy would then stroll across the street to Khan's.

The next morning, he confirmed his appointment with the insurance manager of the Hong Kong and All Asia Shipping Company. He was to settle a client's claim for saltwater damage to three containers and twelve trucks which had been shipped between decks. Twenty-four hours caught in a raging typhoon in the South China Sea had wreaked havoc on the cargo.

He then set off for Khan's Rug Emporium. The taxi ruse worked again, and he was soon shaking hands with Ali Khan himself.

"My dear Mr Tomlinson, how nice to see you again. You have chosen an auspicious day to come to my shop. I have just obtained a selection of the most exquisite Kazak prayer rugs." He waved his hand towards the rear of the shop.

"Ali, my friend, I just work for the insurance company, I don't own it. I want a nice Belushi, three millimetre pile, dark reds into purples, medium size. It is for a friend."

Khan summoned an assistant and pointed to a pile of carpets about a metre high. It was rumoured that at any one time, Khan owned more than two thousand carpets.

"Show my dear friend some of our best Belushis. Mr Tomlinson is a connoisseur."

That night he went to his favourite brothel. He had known Madam Sue Hong for more years than he cared to remember.

"Mr Toms, my number one customer," she beamed as she greeted him. "Long time, no see. Why you keep Sue waiting so long, you naughty man?" Tommy was amazed at the woman's ability to recall names. It certainly was a gift in her line of work. She also knew her customers' tastes, ensuring that all their encounters had happy endings.

Tommy would not have awakened so relaxed the next morning had he known that there had been a power cut in the area of Kings overnight.

Lynda Osborne could not make her usual early cup of tea, and had to wait until almost nine o'clock before the power was restored. She had breakfast before going to get her paper in.

The headline was stark: MASS MURDERER STRIKES KINGS. THREE DEAD

Her chest heaved as she read the awful report. It was terrifying enough for poor Jean Adams to be murdered in her bed, but now Maria Luzzo's son had been murdered. The police were suggesting that the same killer was responsible for Alan Luzzo's death as well, and rumours were now circulating that in Alan's case, the killer had murdered the wrong man. Lynda didn't know what to think. She wished that Tommy was here to share her fear. Trying not to panic, she got up to check her back door and to secure her front door, even though she had done it when she went out to get her paper. It was then that she noticed that Tommy's door was slightly ajar.

At first she hesitated at the thought of an intrusion, but then she swung the door open. It was, after all, her house, she rationalised.

There was nothing out of the ordinary to see. The room was immaculate, but when she gingerly peered into the wardrobe, she found that apart from a trench-coat and one starched shirt, it was almost empty.

She assumed, correctly, that Tommy had taken all his other clothes with him.

The large blue-grey metal cabinet dominated one side of the room. It was obviously locked, so she didn't try the handle. On the top of it stood a large magnifying glass on a fixed stand. Then she noticed a rather pungent musty smell. She couldn't be sure, but thought that maybe the cabinet contained some precious old books. With a window open for a few minutes, the odour soon dissipated.

She found an email on her iPad from U3A, advising all members of an emergency meeting the following afternoon, when the police would have an open forum for members.

The next morning, a locksmith fixed the lock on Tommy's door, explaining that in the power cut, the backup battery had probably failed, tripping the door mechanism. He installed a new battery and checked her smoke alarms.

"You were lucky to catch me, luv. I think that the installed password should work, if not let me know. I'm flat out installing new locks all over town. I hate to say it, but these local events are good for business. I will send you a bill in a few days. Keep locked up now," he added cheerily as he departed.

The special meeting called for U3A members that afternoon soon developed into chaos as the police inspector who was on stage with Detective Clapham and the President of Kings U3A tried to keep order.

When he said that the investigation was "making progress", Ron Barber (aka 'The Joker') yelled out, "So are my bloody apples, but I won't be able to eat them till summer!"

"For God's sake, be serious Ron. People have been murdered," said the chairman, asking for 'a fair go'.

The Inspector continued, asking the audience to be vigilant and keep their homes secure. Where ladies were living alone, he suggested that they think about moving in with family or friends for the time being. Two or three women began to cry. He went on to explain that there was now a task force of twenty detectives working on the case with others being brought in from further afield.

He also pleaded for patience if U3A members were approached again for questioning.

"Ladies and gentlemen, in these cases I have found that often what has seemed at the time an insignificant piece of information has in fact led to the killer being identified. He will make a mistake, they always do, but we are not waiting for that moment. There may be times in the coming days when we ask for a plain-clothes officer to join your meetings. I am not suggesting that the killer may be one of you, but until we find him, nothing can be ruled out. Please do not hesitate to ring us at Crime Watch, even if you wish to remain anonymous."

The meeting broke up with an undertaking by the President to provide a telephone tree of numbers for members to call if they were uncomfortable or needed support at any time. The general feeling was one of fear and uncertainty.

Chapter Thirteen

On his way to the shipping company, Tommy dropped off some laundry at the Chinese shop he always used. It was famous amongst ex-pats for the sign above the counter, "NoTickee No Shirt."

He always smiled when he saw it.

His encounter with the shipping company went well, confirming his method of personal attendance at claims meetings. He had found that face to face was the best way. There was no room for the usual delaying tactics employed when the negotiations were attempted by emails or phone calls.

The shipping company had agreed to pay ninety per cent of the claim, accepting that their captain had made an error of judgement in setting sail despite the hurricane warning. Tommy didn't inquire, but assumed that the man was no longer employed by the company.

He had carefully timed his visit to Hong Kong to coincide with a particular international auction he planned to attend that night, to be held in the ballroom of the Peninsula Hotel. In his opinion the owners had ruined the reputation of the grand old hotel when they had constructed a concealed bridge as a walkway to an annex across the street. Guests were not in the Peninsula at all, but he supposed what they didn't know couldn't hurt them. They could still tell their friends that they had stayed in the Peninsula, and been whisked around town in one of the hotel's fleet of six Rolls Royces painted in British Racing Green, with drivers in full livery.

The room was crowded, and having registered for the auction, he found an aisle seat. He recognised one or two dealers, but kept his eyes on the catalogue.

When the bidding started it was fast and furious. Two hours, later he walked back to the Miramar quite satisfied that he had been able to purchase three out of the four items he had marked down.

There was a message waiting for him when he picked up his key. It was from the manager of housekeeping. Entering his room, he rang the internal hotel number on the message paper.

The man asked if he had made a mistake by putting a bag of near-new clothes in the rubbish basket instead of the laundry basket. Tommy assured the man that there was no mistake and he no longer wanted the clothing.

Having spent twenty-three years in the hotel laundry department, the man was never surprised at the items guests left for disposal, and thanked Tommy for the call. His cousin who owned a second hand clothing shop would be delighted with the haul, he thought, and it would nicely round out his monthly commission.

Mr Thomas Tomlinson had an uneventful flight home the next day. Mrs O froze when she heard someone turn a key in the front door during the afternoon, but sighed with relief when her boarder walked in smiling. He had a medium size trolley case, and a large brown paper parcel.

"Tommy, you're home, thank heavens. I am so nervous I don't know what to do. There's been another murder while you've been away. The whole town is in a state of fear and confusion."

"There, there Mrs O," he said taking her by the hand. "Why don't you sit down and tell me what's going on?"

For the next four or five minutes, almost without pause, she poured out her summation of the events of the last few days.

"The police are not even ruling out that the killer may be one of our members," she said dabbing a tissue to her eyes. "They have been here questioning me about my whereabouts on the night that poor Alan Luzzo was murdered, because some busybody in U3A said that I had a row with him over the play that he was supposed to be directing for the drama group."

"How awful for you Mrs O. Why don't we have a cup of tea and a chat? You put the kettle on, and I'll put my things away."

When Lynda came back with tea, Tommy was looking puzzled.

"Mrs O, has someone been in my room? I think the lock has been tampered with. I placed a small piece of tape on the top of the door when I went away and it has pulled loose."

"Oh yes Tommy, that was me. There was a power cut you see, and the door opened somehow. The locksmith I called said something about a backup battery. Anyway, I checked to see that everything was ok. I must say your room is so tidy."

"So you supervised him, the locksmith, I mean?"

"Of course, I mean you never know with tradesmen."

Tommy gave an almost imperceptible sigh of relief.

"You did the right thing, Mrs O. Now I thought that your rug in the lounge was looking a little faded, so I bought you a new one. I hope you like it."

With that he stood up and used a pocket knife to cut the string around the brown paper package. He spread out the carpet with the afternoon sun coming through the window catching the rich shades of reds and purple he had chosen.

Lynda had never seen such a piece in anyone's home that she knew. She thought it was magnificent.

"Oh Tommy, how beautiful and so tasteful. I don't know what to say. Thank you so much."

"My pleasure, Mrs O, my pleasure."

Lynda bent down to feel the pile. She would invite some U3A friends around for tea very soon, she decided.

"So then, Mrs O, the police have not caught anyone yet? No suspects?"

"No Tommy, there is so much rumour around, I don't even know whether to believe anything that the newspapers are saying. The police seem very vague. They say that they are following lines of inquiry, whatever that means."

"Well Mrs O, we must be vigilant until this person is apprehended. Of course he will eventually be caught. The police often know a lot more than they reveal in the early stages of an investigation."

Lynda wasn't listening. She couldn't take her eyes off her gift. Tommy is such a nice man, she thought. If only she had met someone like him when she was younger.

Chapter Fourteen

The Kings murder investigation had taken on national significance. Clapham and his team were now working under the direct supervision of James Rossiter, a Deputy Commissioner from National Police HQ. With the approval of the local vicar, he had ordered that a fully functional and dedicated investigative unit be put in place in the church hall on One Mile Road. Now there were thirty detectives and senior constables assigned to the case. They had been brought in from precincts often well away from the Kings area, because of some particular specialised experience. With growing public pressure being constantly re-ignited by speculative stories with very little by way of substance, the police were almost in a state of siege.

Ms Marion Steinmeyer, a specialist in criminal profiling, had been sent on loan from the FBI headquarters in the USA, after a special request was made by the Minister of Police to the American Embassy. Her CV showed that she had a PhD in criminology from the University of Maryland, and with twenty years service, was State Deputy Director of Forensic Investigation. She was forty-three years old.

Detective Clapham was teamed with her in a supporting role because of his extensive local knowledge. This was the first time in his career he had worked alongside such a highly qualified professional in an investigation. It put him on a fast learning curve, which was to stand by him in later years.

At their first meeting, after the introductions, it was decided to be on first name terms.

"Marion, have you dealt with a mass murderer operating in such a closed circle as we appear to have here?" he asked.

"Guy, lesson one,' she replied, smiling. "What we are dealing with here is not defined as mass murder, and we are not looking for a mass murderer. We are looking for a serial killer. There is a subtle difference between the two. Let me explain," she continued, removing her glasses and settling back in her chair. "Mass murderers go for the big hit. With them it is all or nothing. Take the Columbine Massacre for example, and the awful shooting in Dunblane, Scotland, where Thomas Hamilton shot dead sixteen children before killing himself. The killer is seeking maximum attention, media exposure and notoriety. They revel in it. Unfortunately in recent years, particularly in the USA, they have become not natural-born killers, but natural-born celebrities, as explained so well by Professor David Schmid of Buffalo University. But, by comparison, they get not so much press in the British Commonwealth.

"Now, our serial killer. He is the more dangerous of the two. He values anonymity, obscurity, and normality. The last thing he wants is publicity. He wants to continue his grotesque game while melding into society, looking just like your next-door neighbour or the man at the bus stop. Believe me Guy, these sickos see all this as a game."

"One more question, and forgive me," said Clapham, taking her pause as the chance to ask. "In your experience Marion, have you found that there is any one defining characteristic which serial killers exhibit that makes them stand apart, and that eventually leads to their apprehension?"

"No, sorry, I wish there was, it would make our work much easier. No, in my experience serial killers are caught by a combination of good luck, happenstance, call it what you will, aligned with good plodding police investigation."

"OK, thanks. I have prepared a dossier of all the relevant information that we are working with at the moment. Can I run through it with you?"

"Yes Guy, let's get this creep."

"Well at this stage, what we have is not much. A small piece of adhesive paper found at the scene of the first murder has been positively identified as a stamp hinge commonly used by stamp collectors. Mrs Luzzo, the wife of Alan Luzzo, volunteered when asked that her twelve-year-old grandson was a stamp collector and sometimes brought his album to the house when he stayed over. So maybe it is nothing."

"Is there a specialty shop for philatelists in the town?"

"I don't know."

"Well that seems a good place to start, don't you think?"

Guy winced. "Of course, you're right, I'll get someone on it right away,"

Left alone, Marion took a memory stick from her bag and began to install a unique algorithm she had invented on the large Apple laptop on the table in front of her. She thought of the program as a kind of DNA for criminals, but one which did not need physical samples to be successful. All she needed to eventually reach a threshold of perception was a series of simple attributes tested against a list of possible suspects. For a start, she planned to have all the members of Kings U3A fill in a simple questionnaire about their likes and dislikes, and multiple choices about how they saw themselves. Ten questions in all. Those thought not capable of being involved through age, infirmity, or ill health would be excluded.

The next step would be to ask relatives to rate their family members, with a slightly different set of questions, with traits, opinions, and attitudes to various topics of interest added. Matters of privacy would be addressed, along with promises of confidentiality. In previous cases where she had employed this methodology, people had willingly co-operated, with a feeling of community spirit. They had all wanted to play their part in catching the killer.

Clapham came back to her table. It was one of eight trestle tables set up around the room for use by the team. At one end of the room were two large whiteboards, and a third displaying a map of the immediate area of the investigation.

"News, Marion," he said. "An investigation of the contents insurance on the home of Mrs Jean Adams, the late wealthy widow, has turned up a very interesting puzzle. The only item not accounted for is her late husband's stamp collection, which, and get this, was valued shortly before his death at over one hundred thousand pounds. If theft was the motive in the Adam's case, then what was the motive in the other two?"

Chapter Fifteen

The editor of the *Kings' Herald* had never been so excited. He had been up all night, and assisted by his wife and Barry Smart, his cadet, he had managed to cobble together eight pages to go to press. To make up some of the spaces on pages which may have been blank, he used existing advertisements, which would be free to his past supporters. The headline he chose was stark:

'SADISTIC KILLER IN OUR MIDST!'

The narrative was heavily laced with strong language; 'merciless, savage, mysterious, cold blooded, beastly, and panic-stricken' as a sample.

Then there was the editorial column, where the editor posed questions for the police, and speculated, along with the now common assertion, that the killer might possibly be found in the ranks of the local U3A.

Barry Smart hammered out all the local theories that he had heard as copy for his 'Out and About' column. The wildest story doing the rounds was that the motive for the killings was a secret love affair between Alan Luzzo and Jean Adams. It had been discovered by Luzzo's son, Christopher. He had killed them both to protect his mother from the scandal, and then took his own life in an act of remorse.

But competing for stories were reporters from the national media. A TV transmitting truck had been set up on a private property directly opposite the church hall, and a police cordon had been set up to keep order for the staff working inside.

Barry was preparing to leave for the hall to join the throng when he answered a call on his cell phone.

"Is that you Barry?" asked the voice.

"Yes, who is this?"

"Barry, it's me, Sam Cook. I've got a story for your Out and About column."

Barry caught his breath. Cook owned a shop in the town called Collectibles and sold old books, coins and stamps. Barry had been trying to sell him advertising space for more than six months.

"Yes Mr Cook, what is your story about? We are very busy here with all the pressure for news which is being generated by the murders."

"I can't tell you over the phone Barry, but it may be connected to them. If you can come to the shop, I can reveal something that you will find interesting."

"I'll come over right away Mr Cook, and thanks."

The traffic was as heavy as Barry could ever remember it. There seemed to be more cars with out of town number-plates than those of residents, and he noticed that these were the vehicles which were being driven faster. He wished he had worn his crash helmet, but had left the office in such a hurry that he forgot it. He had urgent business on his mind.

Collectibles had that particular musty odour that only old books can produce. Mr Cook always wore a green dustcoat, and as he was approaching retirement, a fact that was reinforced by his long white hair, Barry knew that he was from another age. Nobody wore green dustcoats these days.

"Hello there young Barry, I hope you haven't been speeding on that imitation Harley of yours."

"I wish," said Barry. "Anyway Mr Cook, what's up? You said that you had something of interest for me?"

Cook glanced around his shop, but they were alone.

"Barry I am not one to gossip, but with all the rumours around, I have been thinking about one of my regular customers who has been acting a bit strangely over recent days. You know, kind of furtive and nervous, as if he has something on his mind. Usually he is pretty cheerful."

"Go on, I'm all ears."

"Well you see, he has been asking about some really rare stamps. Not the kind you would ever find here. They are well out of my league. He said the price was not the issue so much as the rarity. That was what he was after. He seemed to think that some were about to come onto the market."

"Mr Cook, you haven't told me his name." Barry was getting impatient.

"Well Barry, as I said, I'm not one to gossip, but it was Ron Barber, the insurance agent."

Their conversation was interrupted by the arrival of a customer.

Barry took the opportunity to leave. He smiled at the man who had entered, but the man just scowled at him, and began perusing some of the bookshelves. Barry didn't recognise him. Turning back to Cook, he said, "Thanks Mr Cook, I'll think it over."

On the third try his scooter belched and fired into action. He didn't notice that Mr Cook had already closed the door to his shop, and reversed the OPEN sign to read CLOSED.

As he was riding back to the newspaper office, Barry recalled what his boss said each time he reported that he had been unable to sell any advertising space to Sam Cook.

"Barry, you are dealing with an enigma," he would say. "Cook never has any money to pay for drinks at the club, and constantly moans about the cost of living, yet he has a late model Lexus, and takes more holidays than a schoolteacher. His wife left him years ago, but he is seen from time to time in the company of some attractive women. I'm buggered if I know how he lives, but it can't be from that old stuff he hoards. They say he has a dilapidated annex out the back, which is also full of crap."

Chapter Sixteen

Guy Clapham had not slept the previous night and was sitting at his temporary desk wondering just when, or if, he might get that vital clue that all investigators dream about which would crack the case.

His phone vibrated, jolting him into the present.

"Detective Clapham?"

"Yes, Clapham speaking."

"Detective, this is Dr Carla Davis from the forensic lab. We have discovered two items in the car involved in the Luzzo case which we think will interest you. Our analysis is that a melted glass object from under one of the seats is the remainder of an item used by amphetamine addicts."

"Yes, Ms Davis," replied Clapham, "but how can you be sure it isn't just the remains of a Coke bottle?"

"I was hoping you would ask," she said, in a voice full of confidence. "The glass we have analysed is of a special heat-treated type not commonly available. It is lab quality."

"Are you telling me that Luzzo was using P, it caught fire, and he burnt to death?"

"That's for you to determine, Detective, but it's possible. Now the next item is a door key, which we assume had fallen down against the side of the console. It's a Yale, and we have managed to capture the number on it."

"That's fantastic news," said Guy. "When will the post-mortem report be ready then?"

"Tomorrow, I expect. If the body shows traces of amphetamine or other drugs, then the details will be in the report. Anything else, Detective?"

"No thanks, not at the moment. You people do great work."

She thanked him, and rang off.

Clapham walked over to where Marion Steinmeyer was sitting staring at the computer screen on the table in front of her. He quickly relayed his conversation from forensics to her.

"Well now, there's a new dimension," she said, "but not so unexpected. After all, there doesn't appear to be any corner of the western world these days where someone is not using ice, or P as you call it here. In my experience, availability means dealers. Do you have any on your books, Guy?"

"We have charged one or two suppliers in the last six months, but they were only minor players. One idiot blew up his garage last year, trying to cook up some ingredients to make P from a recipe he found on the internet."

"What about the key?"

"Well, we will do the obvious and check his house and other places that he might have frequented. I'll let you know."

She tapped her keyboard. "Thanks Guy. In my business every little snippet of information is another rung up the ladder to the answer. By the way, I have been thinking about your question the other day about anything that defines a serial killer. There is one possibility."

"What's that?"

"Well there is a tendency for them to be rather 'hands on'. That is, they tend not to use firearms in their killings."

"Thanks, Marion. Now you have got me wishing our maniac had used a gun."

The next morning Clapham got the post-mortem report on Christopher Luzzo. He read, with a growing sense of alarm, that the death was no accident. The pathologist had determined that Luzzo's neck had been broken. Therefore it seemed obvious to Clapham that the killer had intended the fire to destroy all the evidence of the crime. The report went on to note that there were also traces of amphetamines in the blood samples taken from the body, which confirmed his information from the previous day identifying the melted glass in Luzzo's car. He thought again about Steinmeyer's comment regarding availability and dealers. Was Luzzo a dealer or just a user? Here was another line of enquiry for his team. The code numbers on the key which had been recovered were spelt out. He made a mental note to get one of his team to get a replica made and start checking possible places where it may have been used.

What was the link between Christopher Luzzo's death, and those of his father and Jean Adams, other than the fact that they had all suffered mortal injuries to their necks?

As he read on, he came to the clear conclusion that if the killer was not trying to hide some terrible secret, then he was killing just to satisfy some evil and inexplicable urge. Either way, the killer was brutal, but very efficient, because as yet, Clapham had to admit, neither he nor his team had come up with anything meaningful in the way of evidence.

He handed the report to Steinmeyer.

"Here's some light reading, Marion. I'll call a briefing meeting in one hour."

The woman sensed from Clapham's manner that reading the report would reveal only bad news for the team.

Chapter Seventeen

Morris Kincaid decided that as the president of Kings U3A, it was his duty to show leadership to the group's members. Two members of his committee had rung him suggesting that the meeting scheduled for the next day should be delayed, but he refused.

As arranged, the nine members of the committee arrived at his home the next afternoon. They were all familiar with the agenda, but Kincaid often had to limit members' opinions to keep the meeting within the two hour target that he had set. He hated gossip at meetings. He had been a committee member for four years before becoming president, and had unhappy memories of meetings getting out of control and wasting time on trivia.

He opened the meeting with a short acknowledgement of the trauma all members were feeling associated with the murders.

"Despite these horrors," he said, "it is incumbent on this committee to carry on the business of U3A as usual."

He then asked the secretary to read the minutes of the last meeting. These were quickly approved, and the meeting moved on to the financial report.

Charlie Morris had been asked to take over the position of treasurer following Alan Luzzo's death.

"Mr Chair," he started, only to be interrupted by Kincaid.

"Charlie, please don't refer to me as a chair. If bloody PC rules, then call me a sofa, then I will be more comfortable."

Charlie smiled, and ducked the issue.

"Ok, Morris, I get it," he said. "I have had a look at the accounts, but there is a bit of an anomaly which I haven't sorted out yet."

Sam Cook glared down the table.

"Christ, Charlie, you used to be an accountant. We are not talking about the books of the Ford Motor Company. What could be wrong? Luzzo kept them on the back of an envelope."

"Sam, please give Charlie a chance," said Kincaid. "We should be grateful he has agreed to step into the breach at short notice."

Sam folded his arms and his cheeks reddened, but he didn't reply.

Glancing at Kincaid, Charlie continued.

"Well according to the accounts, we should have something like fifteen thousand pounds in accumulated funds. This is showing as ten thousand pounds as an interest-bearing deposit, with a further five thousand four hundred and thirty-one pounds in the current account."

"Yes, yes, we all know that," said Cook. "Why don't we do something useful with it, instead of just letting it sit there? We should give it to a school or something."

Kincaid was furious. "Sam, for God's sake shut up and let's hear what Charlie has to say."

"Don't tell me to shut up Kincaid, I don't like threats."

The rest of the committee made it clear that they wanted to hear Charlie out.

"Well the point is, the money is not in the bank accounts according to the statements I got from the bank this morning. There is five hundred pounds on deposit, and seven hundred and thirty-one pounds in the current account," he said, "which means, by my arithmetic, we are fourteen thousand two hundred pounds short."

Sam Cook exploded, slamming his fist on the table.

"You mean some bastard has stolen our money?"

"Please Mr Cook, control yourself," said one of the ladies. "You frightened me."

"Yes, Sam, let's keep calm and talk about this," said Kincaid.

"Talk, talk, talk, that's all this bloody useless committee ever does," exclaimed Cook.

"Why are you so aggressive today, Sam?" asked Ron Barber, the group convenor. "Dust from your books getting up your nose?"

"I've had a gutsful of you lot. I'm out of here," said Cook with eyes blazing as he stood up, tipped over his chair and strode out of the house.

"Well I never," said the lady who had been frightened. "What a most unpleasant man. No wonder his poor wife left him."

Exasperated by the disturbance, Kincaid stood up. "Look folks, let's adjourn for a few minutes and have some tea or coffee. My wife has laid out some refreshments for us," he said, pointing to the dining room. "Life in Kings used to be so predictable, but these days I feel that some as yet unexplained evil has entered the district."

Later, when they reconvened, it was agreed that the question of the missing funds would be kept within the committee, pending further investigation.

Chapter Eighteen

James Rossiter, the Deputy Commissioner of Police, turned off his cell phone. His conversation with the Minister of Police had not gone well. He had intended to brief the minister on the latest killing before his scheduled press conference at 10.a.m. that morning. The response he got was that the minister had no intention of announcing the possibility of a third death without a clear confirmation of all the facts. The man had added that he needed enough evidence within the next twenty-four hours to be able to make a public statement confirming that 'several strong lines of inquiry were being investigated, and that the residents of the King's area could expect an early arrest.' In the meantime he was cancelling the press conference for that day.

By the time Rossiter reached the Kings operational centre he was feeling pressure like never before in his long career. In his view, politicians were driven not by the public good, but by the timing of the next election, which was now only three months away. The slogan 'Fighting Crime to Protect You' would soon be emblazoned on billboards all over the country along with a powerful photograph of the present Minister of Police posed with a clenched right fist across his chest.

Clapham opened his briefing meeting by introducing DC James Rossiter who was seated next to him. He quickly summarised the current situation and confirmed that Christopher Luzzo had met his death in the same manner as the victims of the first two killings, by attacks to the neck and throat area.

Referring to the large whiteboard, he used a pointer to show that all three attacks had taken place within a five mile circle of their temporary headquarters.

Then it was Marion Steinmeyer's turn.

She thanked the team for the quick response they had achieved in the collection of nearly eighty per cent of the questionnaires which had been sent out to the members of U3A.

"It is still early days in my task of building a criminal profile which may have some legitimacy in our investigations," she said in a clipped professional tone, "so forgive me if I am giving you information which you already have. On the basis of our present information, it is safe to say that the killer is a male, probably between the ages of twenty to fifty, with a military, gym class, or athletic background involving instruction in one of the martial arts. He is most likely acting alone, and is able to move around the area easily, so he will either have a car or access to one. His modus operandi reflects that he is not only confident in his abilities, but is also strong and agile enough to achieve his objectives. Lastly, there is the question of the amphetamine, or ice as we call it at home, found in the remains of Christopher Luzzo. Identifying suppliers and addicts in the Kings area has now, in my view, become critical to the investigation. Thank you," she said, taking a seat next to Rossiter.

James Rossiter got to his feet.

"Team," he said in a quiet voice, "I will not thank you for your efforts so far, because that will come only after this criminal is caught and punished. The Minister of Police has spoken to me this morning about the case, and the growing concern about it throughout the country." At that moment, each individual member of the team felt that the man's piercing blue eyes were fixed on them.

"I have confirmed with Detective Clapham that all leave is cancelled, and I expect 24/7 attention from you all. Acting as a team, we will catch him. The question is how quickly? Good luck."

A murmur of agreement was heard around the hall. The vicar, seated in the rear, murmured a prayer.

After Clapham had covered the tasks allocated to the various members, now made up of six squads each of four members, chairs scraped, and a general hubbub developed as the meeting broke up.

Chapter Nineteen

Thomas Tomlinson was in his office, daydreaming about his recent trip to Hong Kong, when his desk phone lit up. He picked it up with a gruff, "Good morning."

"Tommy, me old china plate, is that you?" asked the voice with a strong London accent.

"This is Tomlinson speaking," he replied, rather sharply.

"Tomlinson, Bomblinson, Tommy it's me, Mark James, your old shipmate."

"Mark, great to hear from you, but please, remember that I've put the old days behind me. How are you, anyway?"

"I'm fine Tommy, and it wasn't your fault that the bloody harbour pilot in Barbados had drunk a bit too much Appleton's rum when he put your ship on the bloody reef."

"Well the learned board of enquiry thought so Mark, I was the captain, so there you go."

"My sources tell me that these days you are the man when it comes to insurance claims adjustments."

"You having a problem?"

Tomlinson knew that his old shipmate was now a partner in a major insurance brokerage in London.

"Nothing to do with shipping this time old man. It's about stamps," was the unexpected reply.

"Have you just had a long lunch, London style? Did you say stamps, Mark?"

"That's right Captain, stamps, and not just any stamps. In this case about a quarter of a million pounds' worth. What is more, they were stolen during a robbery in your bailiwick. Nasty business – the wife of a former client of ours was murdered for them. Why they were in the house with her, I'll never know."

"I'm an adjuster, Mark, not a bloody sleuth."

"Captain, we need a man on the ground we can trust. Once the truth about the real value of those stamps gets out among collectors, the chances of recovery will be nil. We can stall on the executors of her will who will be chasing a pay-out, but we can't stall on getting them found. And as an incentive, we are offering fifty thousand pounds for their safe return. Have I got your attention, Captain?'

"Yes, Mark, you have my attention, but for Christ's sake, drop the Captain. These days I'm just Thomas Tomlinson, got it?"

"OK, OK, don't get your knickers in a twist. What do you think? Could you take it on? It'll give you something to do while you are waiting for another sorry shipwreck. By the way, do you still belong to The Ancient Mariners?"

"It's called The Old Salts these days, Mark, because the committee thought that the word 'ancient' was disrespectful, you know, bloody PC and all that crap, but we kept the black albatross as our emblem as a mark of respect for the real Ancient Mariner."

"Thomas, my dear friend, I'll email you the details for you to mull over, if you give me your address. Get back to me in twenty-four hours if you are up for it, as they say."

"Mark, stay well, and give my regards to the beautiful Noriko," he said, referring to Mark's stunningly beautiful Japanese mistress.

"I would old man, if I knew where she was. Last I heard she was flying Emirates first class with a bloody pilot, but thanks for the thought."

Thomas gave Mark his email address, and rang off.

It took only a few minutes for Tomlinson to read the notes from Mark's insurance company and decide to accept the challenge. He theorised that his claims adjustment work was a kind of detective work, so why not get involved in some real criminal adventure? Fifty thousand pounds for a little detective work. He smiled an evil little smile. It was time to join U3A.

Chapter Twenty

He always felt secure in the cellar. The specially adapted air-conditioner had reduced the possibility of an explosion to almost zero, and the connection to the chimney, which also had additional filters, meant that any fumes that did escape would be dissipated by the prevailing wind which most days blew across the ridge where the shop was situated.

The old formula had changed over the last few years. It was now far less complicated than in the past. Once the need for the former key ingredients, anhydrous ammonia and red phosphorus, had been overcome, his production method was faster. The market was expanding and he was now well placed to satisfy demand in his area of operation.

His life had changed for the better on that slow day when he had taken down one of his own dusty books from the shelves lining the darker side of the shop. Its title, *War, Chemistry and Innovation*, had attracted him. He had never done anything with his degree in chemistry because shortly after graduation, his father, a widower, had suddenly passed away. As an only child, he had inherited the block of four shops, each with a cellar and an upstairs apartment, that his father had aggregated over his lifetime. Two were rented out, providing a small but steady income. This helped to mask some of the cash movements in his bank accounts. The third shop, which adjoined his own, he had left unoccupied for the time being, as not only was it due for refurbishment, but it also provided some privacy for his activities.

The old book chronicled how it had all started with Pervitin. In 1887 a Romanian chemist working in Germany had isolated a stimulant which became ephedrine in 1893, which was then further synthesised by Japanese chemists in 1919, and by 1937, it had become the all-powerful methamphetamine

Pervitin, which was patented by the German pharmaceutical manufacturer, Temmler Werke GmbH. It was later claimed that they based their marketing programme on the success of the Coca-Cola brand. Every doctor in Berlin was sent a sample of three milligrams of Pervitin, presenting it as a new painkiller. Many became hooked even before they began to prescribe it for their patients. Pervitin was sold over the counter, chocolate coated, in fourteen-milligram tablets, packed in a brightly coloured screw topped tube. The Nazis soon discovered it, and it was given to tank drivers and various units of the Wehrmacht, where recruits were able to operate for two to three days without sleep. By 1940, over two hundred tonnes had been produced, with German frontline soldiers often writing home for more supplies.

Overly aggressive behaviour, ego-boosting, hyper-paranoid, and tragically soulless conduct were all tolerated in support of the war.

He had read only a few pages when he decided to close his shop for the day, and except for a snack for dinner, read on into the night. In the days following he began to accumulate small amounts of ingredients by spreading out his shopping so as not to draw attention to himself. At the same time, he planned how to convert his father's old photographic darkroom in the basement under the annex into a full manufacturing kitchen, where he could practise known methods of synthesis. The production of pure methamphetamine would be a hobby which would test his chemical knowledge. What was the harm in that, he thought?

One month later, he realised that not only had he become addicted to the drug, but his wife Amelia had also fallen foul of the habit. Her formerly quiet unobtrusive character had markedly changed. She now aggressively challenged almost all of his decisions, and flew into unprovoked rages over the smallest incidents.

When he found her dead, probably as the result of an overdose from his latest production, he remained calm. If he reported her death, there was bound to be an official coroner's inquiry, and her addiction would be discovered. He would be questioned and the source of her supply would be sought. No, he decided, that was not going to happen. He had plans, and they were not about to be upset by the silly woman's error of judgement.

The next step was simple. He purchased a large tin trunk at a second-hand shop, and closely following instructions he found on the internet, embalmed her body, placing it in the trunk. There was a small ante-room at the back of his lab, and he placed the trunk in there, covering it with a blanket.

Amelia had come from South Africa, and had no local family connections. When acquaintances asked about her, he would say sadly that they'd had a 'bit of a tiff', and that she had gone back home to stay with her sister. Later, he announced that they had divorced.

Chapter Twenty-one

Sam Cook had joined Kings U3A not long after his wife had returned to South Africa. He was just over the age threshold of fifty-five, and was welcomed as a single man, joining one of the interest groups studying Science and Technology. Having new male members helped to address the ongoing gender imbalance found in many U3A chapters. With a degree in chemistry, he was able to hold his own in the monthly discussions. One of his first presentations to the twelve members of his group was entitled, 'P – the Scourge of Modern Society'.

They were more than impressed with his grasp of the subject, and at the same time grateful that they would now be able to comment very knowledgeably on the topic if the opportunity arose.

Sam reflected on their timid mediocrity, all the while keeping up a show of interest in group proceedings.

At the police inquiry centre, policewoman Louise Banks was tired. She had been seconded to Marion Steinmeyer to collate the questionnaires streaming in from the members of U3A, who were keen to assist in the investigation.

"Marion, I'm intrigued by the whole theory of criminal profiling. I hope you can get it to work here in Kings, and soon. The oldies in the town can talk about nothing else, they are all scared to death."

"I don't blame them," said Steinmeyer. "Everyone should be at least careful, when a serial killer is on the loose."

"So what is important when you are building a profile?"

"Trust me girl, everything is important. But I would like to get a hint of P somewhere, so that I can attach a clue to Christopher Luzzo's death. He was a user. There has to be a connection."

Louise went on checking the names on the U3A list as she ticked off the respondents. Nearly eighty per cent of the members had completed the forms.

Barry Smart was waiting for her at their tiny apartment. She could smell the garlic when she opened the door and was delighted to realise that he had prepared their favourite, spaghetti bolognaise. She kissed him and put her arms around his waist.

"Tella me you are from Italia, Luigi," she said.

"Youa are soa beautiful," came the reply, "you musta be Italian yourself, or maybe your mother isa froma Italia?"

"Sorry, Luigi, she is from Stirling, Scotland. Braveheart country."

"Near enough," laughed her partner. "Let's eat."

Later, with the meal over and half a bottle of New Zealand Martinborough Pinot Noir remaining, the couple shared their couch to watch the TV news.

It was all about the Kings killings.

"Enough already," said Louise, reaching for the TV controller.

With the program turned off, Barry nudged closer to her. "Give me the news as you see it, sexy."

"Go away and behave. I'm tired, but you can pour me some more wine. I can give you a little clue in return. But you have to promise that it was overheard in a bar or it fell off a truck."

Barry handed back her glass of pinot, brimming over.

"You sneaky swine," she said. "You are getting one clue, and that's it."

"Go on, go on, stop bloody teasing me. I'm just a poor reporter looking for an angle."

"You could do worse than investigate just who are the users and suppliers of P in the Kings area."

"Really, what do you have? What do you know?"

"You heard it lover, but not from me. I am going to take a shower and wash my hair. See you later, if you are lucky, and don't touch my wine."

He tried to grab her, but she was gone.

The next day, Barry was in the archive room at the *Kings Herald*, furiously calling up microfiche history to find records of P busts, convictions and any other reporting on the topic. He was making notes on his iPad when Terry Holmes, the editor, walked in.

"What's up Barry?"

"Nothing, Terry, just doing a little research on serial killers."

"Never say nothing, Barry, because any thinking person knows that a cadet in a newsroom is always up to something. You won't find anything about serial killers in Kings, because, thank the Lord, we have never had one, and I've been in the area all my life."

"Terry, what do you think about Sam Cook's information on Ron Barber and the stamps story?"

"I think garbage. It's typical that the locals feel that they are all involved in the case, and gossip rules. It must drive the poor bloody police nuts. Cook must have some reason to raise doubts about Barber. They are both in U3A, as I recall. Maybe Barber crossed him at some time? What we do need is some background on Chris Luzzo. Lots of people loathe and detest car salesmen, but they don't kill them. See what you can find, Barry."

Chapter Twenty-two

Lynda Osborne was delighted when Tommy Tomlinson asked her about the procedure for becoming a member of Kings U3A.

"Why, what a good idea Tommy. And you have picked the right moment because the committee have just announced that they are seeking fifteen new entrants to keep up the membership numbers, replacing those lost through attrition. I'll get you the entrance form today."

Tommy felt that he had accomplished step two of his plan. He had decided not to tell Ms O that he was actually fifty-one, but he knew his face was a well-written page and that he could pass for an older man, meeting the U3A membership age qualification of fifty-five. Step one had been his acceptance of the challenge to make fifty thousand pounds.

Now, he had to expand the connection between the deaths of Jean Adams and Christopher Luzzo to see if the theft of the stamp collection had any relevance.

Guy Clapham had been poring over the report on the death of Jean Adams when he noticed what he thought to be an anomaly in the sequence of events as they were reported.

The report stated that Mrs Adams' cleaning lady had called 101 to report a burglary, not a murder. She had called out to see if Mrs Adams was at home, and got no reply. Why did she not immediately go upstairs to check if indeed her employer was at home or not?

He decided to get a second opinion, and walked over to Marion Steinmeyer's table.

"Hi Marion, spare me a minute?"

"Yes Guy, but you owe me a coffee. Why don't we take a walk to the café on the corner of the block? Everyone swears that they have the best barista in the town."

The coffee was as described, good and hot. Guy explained his problem to her.

"Is the cleaning lady a local, Guy?"

"Good question. No, according to the report, she has only been in the country about eight months on a working visa. She is a forty-year-old Filipina, and speaks good English."

"OK then, would she have known that the stamp collection, now reported missing, had been stolen?"

"She didn't report that at the time. She said that downstairs cabinets had been overturned, and various items were missing, without itemising anything. Once Mrs Adams' body was discovered upstairs, she became hysterical and couldn't answer questions in any coherent way. She couldn't have known that a couple of leather-bound albums in a closed cabinet had any value. Why would she be opening closed cabinets anyway? It was later, when the insurance inventory was checked, that the stamps were found to be missing.

"Guy, get real. Maids, cleaners, housekeepers, from my experience open all cupboards, drawers and jewellery boxes any chance they get. It's in their DNA. They soon find out how much stuff you have and what it's worth. Why don't you bring her in for questioning, and I'll sit in. She will see you as a big foreign cop, but with me in the room, she may relax a little."

"So you want to be a nurse, a student, or a secretary?"

"Don't be chauvinistic. What you see is what you get. I'm an American colleague."

"Of course you are, I knew that," replied Guy. "I'll get her in."

Alice Delgardo feared authority, especially the police. Her son Rikki had been severely beaten while in police custody in Manila, three months prior to her leaving to work overseas. His crime was that while riding his motor scooter, he had clipped the side of a roadside stall while trying to avoid a child who had run in front of him. Goods were scattered from the stall, and some broken. It transpired that the stall owner was paying the usual protection money to the police, and wanted redress. Alice had paid a large part of her savings to get Rikki released.

Prior to the interview, Guy had contacted the employment agency that Alice had named in her statement. They confirmed she had a valid work visa and a first class reference from the Manila Golf Club where she had worked as a maid.

Now, she was seated on a hard and uncomfortable steel chair in an interview room in the Kings police station. Guy and Marion sat opposite her.

Switching on a recorder, Guy explained that she had been summoned for questioning as part of the ongoing investigation into the death of Mrs Adams.

"So Ms Delgardo, why did you come to this country?" he asked in a quiet voice.

She hesitated, avoiding eye contact.

"Sir, I came for the money. Money here is much better than in Manila, and I want to save enough for my son to go to university."

"So what are you doing now that Mrs Adams is dead?"

"Sir, her daughter has asked me to continue for a few weeks, while poor Mrs Adams' estate can be settled."

Marion Steinmeyer leaned forward. "Where are you living at the moment, Ms Delgardo?"

"As I said in my statement, ma'am, I am boarding with a Catholic family from my country, who are resident here."

"Are you addicted to any drugs Alice, recreational or otherwise?"

"No, ma'am, drugs are a blight on my country, but I don't agree with the policies of our new President who is encouraging vigilante action as a means of control of the problem."

Guy pushed back his chair a little, folding his arms.

72

"OK Alice, that's all very admirable, but let's get down to business. Who do you think murdered Mrs Adams and stole the stamp collection?"

"Sir, I don't know."

"Did you know that there was a valuable stamp collection in one of the downstairs cabinets, Alice?"

"No sir. At the Manila Golf Club, anyone opening a member's locker or cupboard in the residential annex was dismissed on the spot. I have kept to that rule here."

"Did Mrs Adams have any strangers visit the house while you were there Alice? Think hard now, it's important."

"Well there was a group of nice Mormon boys one day, but Mrs Adams did not invite them in. Then was a group of ladies from U3A who came for a meeting and afternoon tea."

"Yes, anyone else?

Alice stared at the ceiling for a moment. She wondered why the naked bulb had no shade.

"Alice, pay attention, anyone else?"

"Well sir, not really, only that smart young man who sold Mrs Adams her new Mercedes."

"Can you remember his name, Alice?"

"Yes, it sounded like Mr Lotto, he came two or three times. The last time, he brought flowers for Mrs Adams, and took the car away to be washed. I thought that it was clean enough."

"Alice, do you mean the man's name was Luzzo?"

"Yes sir, forgive me. You are right, it was Luzzo. That's Italian, isn't it? He didn't look Italian."

"Alice, were you ever tempted to take something from the house, or was something found to be missing while you were working there?"

Alice thought for a moment.

"There was one thing, but it's rather silly."

"Alice, in a murder investigation, nothing is silly," said Marion. "Please tell us what it was."

"Ma'am it was a front door key. Mrs Adams always kept a spare on a hook in the hallway. I have my own key. I told her it was not good to do that, but she just laughed. A few days before she was killed, she said the key was not on the hook and asked me if I had taken it, but of course I hadn't."

"Ok Alice, that is all for now, you can go. Thank you for coming in."

"Thank you, sir and ma'am, you could teach police in my country how to behave."

Marion showed her out, and returned.

Guy remembered the key found in Luzzo's car. Could it be, he wondered?

"Marion, if Luzzo stole the key, it means that the theft of the stamps may not have been just a random burglary, but a premeditated one, gone wrong. But why kill the Adams woman?"

"Because Guy, she must have recognised him on the night of the burglary. If he had a key, maybe he slammed the door or put a light on. Amateurs sometimes do silly things, you know. He finds her on the stairs, panics and strangles her, and puts her back on her bed. Note, she was not in the bed when she was found."

Guy rested his chin on his hands, elbows on the table.

"Then how's this for a theory, Marion? Luzzo is commissioned to steal the stamps for a third party who then kills him, and takes them?"

"It's possible. Maybe he was repaying a debt or being blackmailed. Remember he did have some money troubles in the past."

"That would make the poor bastard a real cat's paw then."

"Excuse me Guy, but what in the name of Creation is a cat's paw? The English language often holds little surprises for Americans like me."

"It means doing someone's dirty work for them. I first heard it from an old hand when I first joined the force. You can have it for nothing," he grinned.

"Alright I get it,' said Marion. "So someone in the town badly wanted the stamps, but not badly enough to risk showing themselves in order to do the job. Very neat. You get what you want for free, simply by killing the messenger. That makes it both neat and nasty."

"Luzzo was likely an addict, so maybe he was being bribed with a promise of a few grams of the stuff?" said Guy, arching his eyebrows. "Our man is looking more devious and dangerous all the time."

"Time for me to get back to a little profiling," she said.

Chapter Twenty-three

Sam Cook was delighted to have the stamp collection that he had lusted over ever since he had observed Alfred Adams at a specialist stamp auction. Adams had kept his hand up until all the other bidders in the room had faded. In conversation with other philatelists after the auction, Sam soon discovered that Adams was one of the foremost collectors in the district, some said the country.

He was happy to be able to chat with Amelia these days. Sitting comfortably on the tin trunk, he was able to explain to her just how easy it was to get the stamps. It was unfortunate that Luzzo had held out for a larger amount of P than had been agreed before the theft. Sam's rendezvous with him on the golf course had gone well. It had been a simple matter to park on the road and walk to the spot by the driving range. He had a small rag in his pocket, and a bottle of petrol.

Luzzo had arrived with the albums in his car. Once Sam had sighted them, he caught Luzzo off-guard and felled him with a powerful chop to the back of the neck. Once on the ground, breaking his neck required one twist, and he was dead.

He then recovered the albums, placed Luzzo back in the driver's seat, and closed the door. He stuffed the rag in the petrol filler, poured on the petrol from the bottle, lit a match, and walked away.

Sam was sure that Amelia understood his explanation, but these days she was very quiet, just as he remembered her before she had become an addict. From time to time he did hear her voice, but it was very weak He put it down to the fact that she had been very tired recently.

Then he remembered that he had not done his exercises for the day. He stood up and walked back into his lab and sat at the bench. The twenty-five centimetre solid block of wood wrapped in faded velvet had been part of his life since he was eleven years old. He had come home from school in tears, complaining to his parents that he was being bullied by a boy in his class.

His father had taken him down into the cellar, and put the piece of wood, left over from some building alterations, on his work bench.

"Samuel," he began, "I am going to teach you a trick that will help you stop being bullied. I learned it in the army. Now watch closely."

His father raised his right hand from the elbow, and began a chopping motion, steadily striking the block five or six times.

"I will get your mother to sew some material around it, to soften it a bit. Then you can start. Fifty times a day." He held his hand in front of Samuel.

"See this," he said, pointing to the callused edge of his palm, "Samuel, if you do this for a week or two, I will show you the next step, and after that, I promise that you will never be bullied again. It doesn't matter that you are left-handed, the result will be the same."

Sam smiled as he began his exercises. He remembered with pride the day that he had indeed hit the bully, just the way that his father had shown him. The boy had gone wailing to the school sickbay with a broken collarbone. He said that he had fallen over.

Sam sailed through the remainder of his schooling with a new confidence in his secret weapon.

Chapter Twenty-four

Tommy Tomlinson had always prided himself on getting small details right first time. In his early days at sea he had learned just how easy life could become if you followed this course. So in his small notebook he began to write down all the known facts surrounding the theft of the stamp collection. The three deaths, the families involved, any connections, gossip, opinions gleaned through his U3A meetings, and, as a good seaman, even the weather on the days of the killings.

He was well paid by his employer, but fifty thousand pounds was an incentive that he could not resist.

His application for membership of Kings U3A was speedily dealt with by the membership committee. Mrs O had guided him through the list of interest groups. He decided to join a group studying 'America at War – from The Civil War to The Second World War'. Tommy had always been interested in the American Civil War, and he also reasoned that it would be a safe bet that there would be no women in the group.

How wrong he was. At the first meeting he attended there were seven men and three women present. The convenor of the group introduced him as Tommy, explaining that he was 'in insurance' but only part time, as a kind of hobby.

On that day, the presentation was about Lincoln's tragic death in 1865. He was assassinated by an actor, John Wilkes Booth, only five days after General Lee had surrendered and ended the war.

Tommy felt at home in the group, sure that he could hold his own when it came his turn to make a presentation.

Over morning tea, the conversation mostly dwelt on the seeming lack of progress on the police's part in the murder investigations. Tommy listened with interest to the opinion of a very well-dressed lady with an accent he thought was South African.

"My daughter heard from a friend of hers that drugs are involved. She said that Christopher Luzzo was a drug addict."

"Jan, you should be careful what you say," interrupted the group convenor, Ross Cooper. "It's just gossip. We should wait for the full police report. Think of poor Maria Luzzo."

The woman was not deterred. "Well I'm just saying what everyone in Kings knows, and that is that drugs are everywhere, especially P or whatever they call it."

"Quite right," observed one of the men. "It has become a scourge, much worse than heroin or cocaine, they say."

Tommy thought it was time to join in the chatter.

"I can't understand why the police can't just offer rewards for information from the addicts to find the suppliers," he said.

"Simple, old man," said another of the group. "If addicts give up their suppliers to the cops, then they will not be able to get drugs for themselves. It just wouldn't work. I have a friend who is a psychiatric nurse working in a rehab clinic, and she says that there is a lot of intimidation suffered by the addicts."

Tommy frowned, but didn't pursue the topic. He was studying the group, trying to imagine if the killer may have been standing right next to him. They all looked so normal. He decided that looking for a serial killer in a crowd was a bit like guerrilla warfare – the enemy didn't wear a badge or a uniform. Besides, no one had as yet suggested that the killer was a U3A member.

Mrs O was waiting for him in the afternoon and insisted on interrogating him about the various members of his group. Tommy was pleased to get back to the quiet of his office, having taken a half day off. He had already decided that the fastest way to find a P dealer was to try and buy the stuff himself.

Chapter Twenty-five

The police inquiry into the Kings killings were not making the kind of progress that Deputy Commissioner James Rossiter had promised in his last conversation with the minister. The pressure for results was affecting all those involved. Guy Clapham just wished that politics could be kept out of the day's activities.

He was with his team reviewing the case for what felt like the twentieth time, when his cell phone vibrated. Excusing himself, he stepped out to the foyer.

"Detective Clapham, this is Dr Rule. I spoke to you about the recent post mortems."

"Yes, Dr Rule, have you found something more?"

"Well I don't want to get your hopes up, but I noticed something very unusual as I reread my notes. I have come round to the view that your killer may be left-handed."

"Go on," said Clapham, with a sudden burst of excitement.

"The way the necks have been broken in the case of the two males, from an angle, suggests a dominant left hand approach. I can't prove it, but I thought that the possibility might interest you?"

"It certainly does, Doc, can I come and see you in town?"

"Anytime, Detective. I'll be pleased to flesh it out. Sorry, no pun intended," replied the pathologist, smiling to himself.

Guy had always thought that those working in Rule's profession were entitled to some levity, just to remain sane.

His cell phone vibrated again.

"Guy, it's O'Neil here, I'm the desk sergeant at HQ. Bloody Rossiter is here with some other suits, and wants you here pronto. They just walked in the door as I was taking the call."

"What call?" asked Clapham.

"We've had another one, mate. Found in his back garden of all places. Broken neck."

"Save it, O'Neil, what's the address?"

Clapham's Volvo was an unmarked car, until he turned on the flashing blue lights in the front and rear, and the siren. He sped to the address which was on the outskirts of Kings, near a motorway onramp. Rossiter could wait, he thought. At this moment his presence at the crime scene was more important.

Members of the serious incident squad were already taping the surrounds of the property when he arrived. A constable directed him to the rear of the property. The house was a beautifully maintained Tudor-styled home, with raked pebble driveway and paths. The gardens were well-tended.

A woman was sitting on a white wooden garden chair quietly sobbing as he approached. A policewoman had a hand on her shoulder. Several yards away, lying sprawled across a square raised timber herb garden, was the body of a man, lying on his back, arms outspread.

"What have we got?" asked Clapham as he approached the three policemen gathered around the body.

"It's bad news Guy," said the nearest man. "The deceased has an obviously broken neck. No other signs of violence. Looks like the bastard has struck again. His wife found him when she came to check why he had not come in for his morning tea. Poor woman, she was the one who made the call."

"Where's the Doc?" asked Guy.

"On his way now Guy, with the rest of the forensic team."

Clapham stared at the body. He thought that from the evidence of white hair, the man may have been in his late sixties. From his clothing it was clear that he was dressed for gardening. A small trowel and a bag of fertiliser lay near the body. His head was twisted more than ninety degrees to the right.

"Listen up," he said, thrusting his hands deep into his pockets. "We speak to no one, no speculation, no comment on the cause of death, nothing. We must keep it tight until I can inform Rossiter, and he can decide on a press briefing. Understand? Extend the cordon around the entire property."

They nodded.

He turned towards the woman sitting in the chair.

"This is Mrs Kincaid, Detective," said the policewoman. "She found Morris, her husband, about forty minutes ago."

"Take a statement from her when you think she is ready. I'm going to HQ," said Clapham.

The policewoman hesitated. "Sir, Mr Kincaid was the president of Kings U3A."

Clapham was startled. His mind was in a whirl. He could hardly get the words out.

"Look after her. I am needed back at HQ."

An overwhelming sense of frustration was now beginning to make him doubt his own abilities as a policeman. A homicidal maniac was now killing seemingly innocent citizens right under his nose, and he was, at the moment, powerless to do anything about it.

The scene at HQ was quiet. James Rossiter was sitting with his arms folded talking to Marion Steinmeyer. Three strangers were standing beside him. Members of his team were not ready to make eye contact with Clapham as he approached Rossiter.

"Sir, I have been to..." he began.

Rossiter interrupted him.

"Detective, these gentlemen," he said, waving his arm in an arc, "are from the Inland Security Service, under instruction from the Prime Minister to assist with the investigation. We are instructed to work twelve-hour shifts in rotation until this criminal is apprehended. Follow-ups in cases of burglary, traffic violations, and other minor offences are to be suspended, and all staff are to be made available to assist in the inquiry as required."

Clapham nodded. He sensed that the political intervention he had feared was now about to overshadow his real effort, and that of his team, to catch the killer.

"Sir, Mr Morris Kincaid, the president of Kings U3A, has just been found dead in his garden. First indication is that the murderer has struck again."

Chapter Twenty-six

Tommy Tomlinson heard the news of the latest killing while he was driving to an appointment with a client. He pulled over and sat, stunned, listening to the report.

The announcer said the name of the dead man was being withheld until relatives could be advised, but local sources had it that the dead man was the president of the local chapter of Kings U3A.

"Bloody hell," he mouthed the words without actually getting them out.

He decided that Kings U3A was now under siege. A killer was lurking in plain sight, and despite the best efforts of the police, he or she was able to continue creating mayhem undeterred. He, Tommy Tomlinson, would for the time being forget about the fifty thousand pounds. In order to protect Mrs O, and all the other U3A members, he felt he would make it his responsibility to stop the killer.

Remembering his appointment, he drove off again, hoping that it would not take too long as he had already begun to form a plan of action. He still missed the satisfaction that being responsible for a ship and its cargo had brought him. If he could bring this man to justice it would go some way to restore the reputation that he had left behind him on that fateful night when the ship under his command had struck the reef.

Barry Smart was always the first person to answer the phone at the *Kings Herald*. The editor could not afford a receptionist, so this duty fell to the person nearest a phone. Barry was always ready for a lead which would produce a story for his Out and About column.

"Could I speak to Mr Smart, please?" said a male voice.

"This is Barry Smart speaking, what can I do for you?"

"Hello Mr Smart, I have been following your stories in the *Kings Herald*, actually in your special column. I would like to meet you about a proposal that I have in mind which may be of interest to you."

God, thought Barry, another nutter with a theory about the killer?

"What kind of a proposal would that be?" he asked.

"One which could earn you ten thousand pounds."

"I'm interested," Barry blurted out. "Who are you?"

"My name is Tomlinson, Tommy Tomlinson. When can I meet you?"

They agreed to meet the next day at the café near the temporary police inquiry centre.

Barry couldn't sleep that night. Ten thousand pounds would allow him to buy the ring he had been promising Louise for months. He prayed that Tomlinson was not going to ask him to participate in something illegal.

Chapter Twenty-seven

The Goh Coffee café had never been busier. The police activity in the area meant the barista Mr Goh had employed was constantly in demand.

Tommy was already seated when he noticed the young man on a motor scooter pull up outside. Barry had mentioned it as a means of recognition. He stood up and motioned to Barry to join him at the little table.

"Hello Barry, I'm Tommy. Thanks for coming."

"No problem Tommy, pleased to meet you," he said holding out his hand.

Barry prided himself on his ability to judge people. He immediately decided that Tommy was not a nutter. If he was, then he was the best dressed nutter he had ever heard of.

With coffee ordered, Tommy began the conversation.

"I have been keeping up with the news Barry. Your paper is doing a pretty good job. Must keep you busy?"

"Sure does, but it's really exciting. Well not exciting that so many people have been killed, but exciting from a journalist's point of view."

"Well, Barry, my proposal is that we more or less form a little team, to do what the police have so far not been able to accomplish. I propose that we commence a parallel investigation."

"Wouldn't that be against the law, Tommy?"

"Of course not. It would be a citizen's initiative in my view, but very confidential."

"But my partner is a policewoman," said Barry.

"How convenient. Let's talk some more, eh?"

To any onlooker, the two men sitting at the little table in the corner could have been a father and son, catching up on family matters. But in the hustle and bustle of the café they went unnoticed as they discussed serial killers.

"But what's your interest, Tommy? The police seem to be busy, they have an army on the case. They will be well ahead of anything that either you or I could discover. They always hold back information, so they may have someone under surveillance right now."

"You may be right Barry, but until they make an arrest the case remains open. What I find really disturbing is that the bastard is amongst us every day. Confident, clever, cunning and utterly ruthless. We need just one little ripple from his activities to alert us. For a start, I think that the trace of P found on Christopher Luzzo's body may be the first stone in the pond. I am going to look for a dealer right here in Kings."

Barry looked puzzled. "I don't see that I can get more info than the police already have, and anyway with Louise being in the police and all, I don't want to get her in any trouble. She's already very sensitive about her position."

"Barry, I am not suggesting that she should spy for us. We are the spies. I am going to write up a kind of log of what is already in the public domain, and look for any threads that may already be there. When I have done that, we will get together and review it. What do you say?"

"Of course I want to help, but where does the money you offered come in?"

"Good man, I was waiting for you to raise the matter," said Tommy gazing casually around the café. "I will give you a starting bonus of one thousand pounds when we have our next meeting, and then one thousand a month until we or the police catch the bastard. If he is caught before we reach the ten thousand pound mark, I will pay you the remaining balance. If he is not caught by then, I will review the situation, but I think we will get him sooner rather than later."

"I'll shake on that," said Barry, reaching across the table, "and I'll see just what extra I can glean from my contacts till we meet again. But there is something that I heard that is not generally known."

"There Barry, you have only been on the payroll ten seconds, and you're already working. What is it?"

It was Barry's turn to peer around the surrounding tables, but nobody was looking their way.

He leaned forward and whispered, "The word is that he may be left-handed."

"Barry, you are a gem," said Tommy.

They exchanged cell phone numbers, before leaving the café.

Barry was already torn between either a ring for Louise, or an upgrade to a Piaggio scooter that he had been studying on the internet.

Tommy thought it would be a good time to open the steel cabinet in his room and check the condition of the 9mm Glock he had kept in his cabin while at sea.

Chapter Twenty-eight

Elaine Russell had been working part-time for Sam Cook at Collectibles for more than three years. She was an avid reader and appreciated the fringe benefit of being able to take home and read any book she wanted. Wednesday to Friday were the busy days, and she worked from 10a.m.to 4p.m. Elaine found Sam to be rather secretive, and their communication centred mainly around the books in the store. He attended to the regular coin and stamp traders in his small office at the rear of the shop. She had noticed that he seemed to spend a lot of time in the cellar, which he kept locked. She suspected he was drinking in there during the day, but as she had never been in there, she could not confirm her suspicions, although she had not noticed alcohol on his breath. He also kept the door to his upstairs apartment locked.

Elaine was at the front desk serving a customer when she heard a thump, followed by a cry for help. She ran to the rear of the shop to find Sam lying on his back, partially covered in books, with the step ladder he had been using collapsed against the shelves. His right leg was contorted at an odd angle underneath him.

When the hastily summoned ambulance arrived, the medics quickly established that Sam had broken his hip, and was in shock.

As he left for the hospital, Elaine asked him what she could do to help him. Sam asked her to put the closed sign on the door and go home until he contacted her.

Left alone, she tidied up the fallen books, picked up the ladder, and took the cash from the till, placing it in the floor safe. Satisfied that everything was secure, she was locking up when a stranger approached.

"Is Sam in there?" he asked.

"No, I'm sorry. He has had an accident and been taken to hospital."

"Well then, can you help me with some stuff?"

"What stuff are you talking about?"

"You know, you stupid bitch, stuff."

Elaine was shocked, but held her nerve. Without waiting or replying, she locked the door of the shop, and walked off.

The man ran after her, yelling for her to stop, so she quickly stepped into the florist's shop on the corner. She knew the florist and asked her to call the police as she was being threatened by a stranger.

Five minutes later, as a police car arrived, the man was nowhere to be seen.

Chapter Twenty-nine

Sam Cook had a fear of hospitals. He would have no control over events, and he could sense that his life was spiralling downwards. This was confirmed when a surgeon and an anaesthetist came to his bedside. He had suffered a sleepless night despite the sleeping pills and pain killers which had been administered to him.

"Mr Cook, we have decided to operate on your hip this afternoon. The x-rays have revealed that you need to have a full hip joint replacement. For that we need your agreement."

Sam snarled at the doctors, "Listen you two, I just want to be patched up and get out of here. I'll wait for the bloody thing to heal."

The surgeon smiled at Sam. "Mr Cook, I don't do patch-ups, and hip breaks don't heal. If you want to spend the rest of your life crippled and in a wheel chair, then that is your decision. Do you have a friend who will push you around?"

"Fuck you."

"Is that a yes or a no, Mr Cook?"

"If you do it, how long do I have to stay in this dump?"

"Maybe five days, then you will be on crutches for up to six weeks. It usually takes about three months for a patient to be fully mobile again."

The other doctor spoke. "Mr Cook, I have noticed a high level of amphetamine in your blood results. Are you a regular user?"

"Mind your own damn business."

"Mr Cook, I don't care if you smoke maple leaves, but I may have to adjust the anaesthetic that I give you."

"Do whatever it takes, just get me out of here."

The surgeon read Sam the statutory disclosure covering the risks involved in the operation, and then asked Sam to sign it.

"Oh, another lefty," he commented as Sam reached for the pen.

At one o'clock the anaesthetist came back.

"Hi there Mr Cook, I am just going to give you a pre-op shot of happy juice to calm you down before we take you into the theatre. I will put a shunt into the back of your left hand, so I can top you up if necessary, okay?"

The doctor noticed that the edge of his patient's hand was unusually calloused, but didn't comment, assuming that he had been a farmer or maybe a forester.

When Sam woke up the next morning, it took him several seconds to realise that he was in a hospital. A nurse was standing next to the bed.

"Hello Mr Cook, pretty sleepy?"

"Give me a glass of water. I am as dry as a wooden god."

"That's not unusual Mr Cook, it's the drugs we use."

Sam drank the water, and drifted off to sleep again.

He awoke again to the clatter of a trolley being wheeled into his room. It was being pushed by a rather jolly overweight lady.

"Are you ready for something to eat, dear?"

"Coffee and toast would be good," said Sam, "and do you have an apple?"

"Of course dear," she replied, fixing a tray to the side of his bed.

"And would you mind passing me my trousers? I need something from my pocket. I think that they must be in that cupboard there," he said pointing at a wardrobe next to the entry door.

When the woman gave him his trousers he quickly removed his wallet and a small sealed envelope.

When she had gone he took a small tablet from the envelope, poured a glass of water from the jug by the bed, and swallowed 8 grams of almost pure amphetamine. One hour later, an athletic young woman wearing a blue track suit bounced into the room.

"Hi Mr Cook, I'm Nancy from the physio department. Time to get you out of bed and teach you to walk again. The surgeon said that your op went well, so congratulations."

"In your dreams woman. Come back tomorrow."

"Now is best, Mr Cook," she said turning back his covering sheet. "Don't panic, I am going to help you."

"Don't you bloody touch me, bitch," he said, raising his left hand.

In a split second the woman had Sam in an excruciating finger hold and was about to dislocate his little finger.

"Naughty, naughty, Mr Cook, we don't want to have an accident, do we now? We call this the chicken wing hold. It's fun, don't you think?"

"If you say so," he muttered. "For Christ's sake let go, you're hurting me."

"And I'll hurt you again if you don't behave." She smiled. "One of my naughty clients even broke his own arm last year. The management are still puzzling over it. I notice that you must be a Dai Kwando fan too, with a hand that heavily calloused. Left-handed, too. I'd better be careful."

Sam decided that walking was a priority, and didn't comment. He did not resist when the ever-cheerful Nancy lifted his legs and helped him sit on the edge of his bed before introducing him to his crutches.

Five days later, having mastered the technique of using them, he was released into the care of Elaine Russell, his employee from Collectibles. She drove him to the shop and helped him into his office, where he insisted on being alone for fifteen minutes. When he came out, he gave her a small parcel to post, and then paid her in cash for the airline ticket to Turin, Italy which she had purchased for him. From there he would be driven by hire car to Stresa on Lake Maggiore, where he planned to quietly rehabilitate himself in luxury, at the one-hundred and fifty-year-old Grand Hotel Des Iles Borromees.

She drove him to the airport, where a ground steward with a wheelchair took over. With a cursory wave to Elaine, he was gone.

He had promised to call her when he was ready to reopen his shop, giving her one thousand pounds, again in cash, to check the shop weekly until his return.

When she stopped to post Sam's parcel, she was puzzled when she noticed he had addressed it to himself at the hotel in Italy. However, she soon forgot about it when she arrived at the local shoe store with one thousand pounds in cash in her handbag.

Murder Comes To U3A

Part II

Chapter Thirty

Almost four weeks had passed since Morris Kincaid's body had been found in his garden. The police investigation was still no further advanced. The media' s attention had been diverted by a sex scandal involving a senior politician, which saw the daily report on what had now been labelled 'The U3A Serial Killer' consigned to page three. Protests by the members of Kings U3A that such a headline implied that the killer was a member of the group went unheeded.

Ten additional uniformed police, with five unmarked cars, were now patrolling the streets of Kings on a twenty-four hour basis. Most of the members of U3A who had been living alone had either gone to stay with relatives or friends, or had left the area to take a holiday. A telephone list had been distributed and a special volunteer committee set up to check on every member at least once a day.

The police, in partnership with a national telecommunication company, had organised a special 222 emergency number for use only by residents of Kings.

Detective Clapham had become part of a national police team overseen by Deputy Commissioner Rossiter and meeting daily to review progress.

"Good morning everyone," he said. "The data being collected for Ms Steinmeyer's profiling is going well. We have identified nine adults in the area who are left-handed, but I still have to point out that the possibility of the killer being left-handed is a theory only. Nevertheless it is another brick in the wall. Finding active P dealers is proving difficult. What is interesting is that in the nearly four weeks since the Kincaid death, our sources report the local supply of P has more or less dried up. This could be because of our increased presence, and the local dealer or dealers have decided to lie low. However, we know with the addicts in the area, demand will not dry up, and maybe other dealers will move into the town. The theft of nearly fifteen thousand pounds from the U3A accounts is worrying, as it points to the former treasurer, the late Mr Alan Luzzo. Our forensic team is still analysing the Luzzo family bank accounts to try to establish any links to the crimes. I am satisfied with the teams reporting on each killing, and urge you all to keep up the good work. We will nail this bastard, however long it takes. Questions?"

Louise Banks put up her hand.

"Sir, it may be significant that at the same time that P supplies have dried up, there have been no further incidents, I mean killings?'

"It could be coincidence, it could be connected. We don't know, but again I urge you all to have these possibilities in front of you all the time. Any more questions?"

There were no more questions, and the teams dispersed to carry on their inquiries.

Clapham sat across from Steinmeyer's desk with his elbow and hand supporting his chin.

"There is something that I am missing, Marion. Why would Alan Luzzo, a retired banker, steal a lousy fifteen grand? In my experience on the fraud squad, when bankers go feral, they go big!"

"Maybe he didn't want any dark transactions to appear in his day to day banking," she offered.

"Blackmail," said Clapham. "Maybe something to do with his wayward son?"

"Possibly, Guy, but remember we have no proof that Alan Luzzo was the thief. How many people could sign U3A cheques? Maybe there was some internet banking involved?"

"The forensic squad are taking their time. I guess we will just have to wait. Any views yet on the left-handed theory?"

"Well if the killer is left-handed, he's in good company. Jimi Hendrix, Obama, Clinton, Bush snr. and Reagan are all noted as being left-handed," she replied.

"Yes, but as far as I know, none of them have retired to Kings," said Clapham with a smile.

Tommy Tomlinson had been meeting with Barry Smart on an irregular basis, so as not to raise any questions about the *Kings Herald* reporter being seen having meetings with Mrs Osbourne's boarder.

Tommy was waiting for Barry in the local park, sitting by a fountain, eating his lunch. He stood up as Barry arrived, hoping his amateur investigator might have some news on the missing stamp collection.

"Hi there young Barry, what's new?"

"Bad news, for me anyway. Louise has been posted out of town on a six-month transfer. Her new station is thirty-five miles away and we will probably have to move."

"It's about time you got off that scooter before you have an accident. Why don't you talk to Louise about getting a small car?"

"I'll think about it."

"Any news on the missing stamps?"

Barry explained that the late Alfred Adams, husband of the murdered woman, was a well-known collector, not only locally, but also nationally. There were more than five full- or part-time stamp dealers in or around Kings, and Barry had spoken to them all but one, Sam Cook, who owned the shop Collectibles. According to the florist on the same block, Cook's assistant Mrs Elaine Russell had told her that he had fallen off a ladder in the shop, and was overseas recuperating from a broken hip. Barry was not surprised to learn that in every other case, the dealers had already been interviewed by the police and had little more to offer.

One of the more experienced philatelists had suggested that the Adams collection would be broken up and sold in small lots over an extended period, which would make them almost impossible to trace.

"Well you keep your ear to the ground Barry," said Tommy. "I have been chatting to some of the local landlords trying to penetrate the drug underground in the area. The general view seems to be that apart from the usual gang activity, there are two or three distributors in the area, one of whom has access to a particularly high grade of P. He is a mystery man. If anyone does know something about him, they are certainly not talking. I sense that since the murder of Christopher Luzzo, there is an ever-deeper feeling of fear amongst addicts, much more than in the general public. The police have let it be known that anyone offering worthwhile information will be well rewarded. However, it is not an offer that they are publicising."

"So what now?"

Tommy looked thoughtful. "We just keep on listening to the gossip, and wait to see if our man has gone to ground. He may already be in jail on some other charge for all we know. It wouldn't be the first time the police have had their man and not known. My bet is he will strike again soon, because some of the research I have seen shows that serial killers see it all as a game. To catch them, you have to play the game, and sometimes you're the cat, and sometimes you're the mouse. It depends who the killer is."

"That Sam Cook who broke his hip has a reputation for being a bit aggressive, according to the florist, and I thought it was a bit mean for him to try to place suspicion on old Ron Barber over the stamps," said Barry.

"Look, in this atmosphere of dreadful uncertainty Barry, there are shadows everywhere," said Tommy.

Chapter Thirty-one

Sam Cook was relieved when the parcel of books arrived at the hotel. He had almost exhausted the small amount of P that he had packed into the hollowed-out book in his suitcase. The Italian customs had not even glanced at the man in the wheelchair as the ground steward had pushed him through the green lane, marked: '*niente da dichiarare*,' Nothing to Declare.

He had already initiated a plan B by approaching the concierge at the hotel. The tall and elegant Italian had brushed some imaginary dust from the brass crossed keys badge on his lapel, when Cook approached.

He had started the conversation by asking the man if he could find someone to walk with him during his stay. First, he explained that walking was necessary to aid him in getting off his crutches as soon as possible. He then asked if the concierge could help him with some painkillers to dull the pain of his recovery from the operation. In fact, he was surprised that he had felt no pain whatsoever, but it was a good story.

When the man came to his room later and saw the roll of notes Cook pulled out, he soon understood what kind of drugs Cook had in mind. The parcel that he had left for Elaine Russell to post had not arrived, and he was becoming agitated at the thought that it may have been intercepted at the border.

The next day he was introduced to Violetta Cavalli, the concierge's daughter, who was to become his 'walking buddy,' as the physio at the hospital had recommended. She was in her early twenties, and was home for a break from Milan University where she was studying English literature.

Cook usually had no patience whatsoever with the antics of the present generation, but he could not dispute that the woman had a strong and happy personality.

As the weeks went by, Cook's confidence in his ability to walk naturally began to return. He had already dispensed with the crutches, and quite enjoyed the reputation he was gaining by walking along the promenades beside Lake Maggiore with a beautiful young woman on his arm. Violetta encouraged him to try to speak a little Italian, but Cook was having none of it, except in the case of restaurant menus. On the odd occasion when he did invite her to lunch, he paid close attention to her translation, because of all Italy's usual attractions, first and foremost he liked the food.

Her father the concierge had introduced him to Adolpho, a fast-talking young local man who drove a Maserati. He kept Cook supplied with the P which satisfied him, although he was convinced that his own product was superior. After two or three deliveries, Cook became very disappointed that Adolpho wanted to double the price of the drug. When he protested, the Italian had called him *'fottuto bastardo inglese'* which from Cook's point of view, was unfortunate.

He made the decision to return home after two months instead of the recommended three months of rehabilitation, because he was satisfied that his old confidence had returned, together with his balance. The fact that his parcel had never arrived also provided a strong incentive to return home, to commence his own manufacturing again.

Unaided, he was walking well and feeling no pain. He could never have been a surgeon. The thought of taking a saw to someone's hip and screwing a piece of metal into place made him sick. He didn't begrudge any fee to the surgeons, they were worth every dollar.

Violetta sobbed as he got into the hire car which would take him back to Turin airport. Cook had tipped both her and her father enough money to keep her in shoes for at least two years, and him in cigars for about the same period.

It was three weeks later that a tourist on the lake promenade spotted a piece of metal shining deep in the clear water. The sun was reflecting on the small chrome trident which is the traditional badge of Maserati.

The post mortem performed on the body which was found when the car was recovered by the Stresa carabiniere showed that the deceased driver, identified as Adolpho Galliotti, had died of a broken neck. The accident report determined that the driver had been speeding and had lost control of his vehicle on a notorious corner. As is the case in many countries, the coroner's report would not be released for at least six months at the earliest.

Chapter Thirty-two

Elaine Russell was a little surprised when Sam Cook rang her to say that he was home early and intended to re-open Collectibles the following Monday.

He was happy to be back in familiar surroundings, and especially pleased to be able to tell Amelia about his trip. It was his one regret that she had not been able to be with him, but he was sure she understood.

There were more than a dozen messages waiting for him, all of them from customers who were desperate to do business with him. Fortunately he had stockpiled enough ingredients to be able to go straight back into production. His one concern during his stay in Italy was that another more aggressive supplier might have moved into Kings during his absence. He would interrogate his customers, just in case.

He was careful to work only late at night, so the fumes from his cooking, which were exhausted by a system of fans to an outlet high on his roof, would not be noticed by the locals.

Tommy Tomlinson was sitting at his desk contemplating the list of U3A members that Barry Smart had managed to extract from a former committee member, on the strict understanding that he would not use it to annoy members with advertising offers and the like. Tommy had decided to concentrate on the male members on the list, discarding for the time being the idea that any female member could qualify as a suspect. That decision had reduced his list of possible suspects to thirty-one.

Barry had passed on the information that the police had an FBI profiler working on the case, so the race was on to see just who would be the first to identify the killer.

He had devised a spreadsheet to accommodate his own findings as he began to accumulate a list of common denominators which were already public knowledge.

What he needed now was a door into the world of P users, their habits and contacts. If only he could manage to open this door, then it might lead him to the killer.

Tommy decided to find out if there was a drug rehabilitation centre in or near Kings. A quick search on Google confirmed that there was one. It was located in a large former farmhouse on the edge of the town.

He introduced himself at the reception desk, handing over his card, and explaining that he had been sent by the insurance company to assess the fire risk in the building, and to confirm that the smoke alarms and extinguishers were all in good order. The receptionist asked him to take seat while she spoke to the manager.

Tommy sat in the small waiting room. There were two other people there, a man and a woman. The woman, wearing a heavy coat and a tattered old pair of trainers, was staring at the floor. The man, wearing jeans and a hoodie, looked up at Tommy.

"How's it going, mate?" he asked.

"I'm fine, thanks," said Tommy.

"Know where I can get some really good stuff then?" said the man.

"Ask bloody Bookman," said the woman, without looking up.

"I would, you silly bitch, but he's gone away." He looked back at Tommy.

"Well mate, what do you say?"

Tommy was hesitating when thankfully, the receptionist appeared and said that the manager was ready to see him.

"You know, don't you, you bastard, but you're not telling, you bastard," shouted the man.

"Don't take any notice," said the receptionist to Tommy. "They are always very aggressive when they are coming down."

Doctor Marie Covic was standing at the window looking out over the remaining acreage of the farm.

"Good morning, you have come about the insurance?"

"That's right," said Tommy, "I should have made an appointment."

"No problem, but I thought the trust committee had arranged all that."

Tommy smiled and lied, "Yes, but I have some forms with boxes to tick as I walk around, it will only take a few minutes."

The doctor sat down. "I see from your card that you are a ship's captain, shouldn't you be at sea?"

"I was at sea for many years, but I had an accident, which put me ashore."

"My uncle was a seaman, in the navy. He has many tales to tell."

Tommy could see that the doctor was up for a chat. Maybe she was having a rough morning with her clients, and needed a little diversion.

"Tell me Doctor, as a matter of interest, is the P problem in Kings worse than elsewhere, what with all these murders?"

"That is what everyone wants to know, Captain, but I don't think so. Anyway, I have to respect client confidentiality. My personal view is that the quality of the drug being supplied in Kings is much higher than elsewhere, and that seems to indicate that there is advanced knowledge of chemistry somewhere in the supply chain."

"I mustn't keep you Doctor, I saw that you have clients waiting. I'll get on with my check, if you don't mind."

"Go right ahead Captain, we want everything shipshape don't we?" she smiled.

Tommy spent ten minutes wandering around the facility jotting down notes in his notebook. Anyone checking would have been puzzled to find that he was writing from memory, a poem about the sea.

His brief meeting with the doctor had confirmed one thing in his mind, and that was the fact that at least one of the P suppliers in the town was very well educated. Enough maybe, to also be the 'cook'. Cutting out the middleman was a basic strategy in any good marketing plan. Vertical integration led to vertical profit lines on any graph.

Chapter Thirty-three

When the police announced that they were closing the temporary headquarters in the local church hall and moving the whole murder investigation back to the main police station, there was outrage in Kings. It was led by the *Kings Herald* newspaper. The editor decided on a provocative headline. 'Police Puzzled by Murderer, Pull Out'.

"They are not really pulling out," Barry explained at his next meeting with Tommy. "Louise said they prefer the headquarters building because of the better facilities there over the long term."

"So they are thinking long term?" said Tommy. "That doesn't bode well for the locals. If anything it will only increase the general level of anxiety, as if it isn't high enough already."

"I agree," said Barry, "but there are no signs of progress, you have to admit."

"Well Barry, let's review what we know. We have a well-educated, probably left-handed killer, who may also be a P user or supplier or both. He may have a connection with Kings U3A, and I suspect he is a loner. I had an interesting exchange with a couple of addicts yesterday. Does the name Bookman mean anything to you?"

"No, why?"

"Well this woman at the clinic yesterday linked P supply, and the word Bookman. I have checked the local directory, but there are no residents by that name in the area. Maybe it's a nickname, most crims operate under an alias, I believe."

"I meant to tell you Tommy, that Louise and I have bought a car. It's an old Toyota Corolla. They say Toyotas go forever, so I hope it's true. We move out this weekend to a new apartment closer to Louise's station."

"Good luck, Barry, I hope the move and the car go well. What happened to the scooter?"

"I sold it to a friend for three hundred pounds. I hope he remains my friend."

"You should never sell things with engines to friends, Barry. Is Louise going to have any connection with the investigation, or is she assisting with normal police duties as before?"

"Just the usual, but she has been nominated to take driver training at the police driving school, and she is pretty excited about that, because not many policewomen get to go there. She said it was because she was a go-kart champion as a teenager. Apparently many Formula One drivers come from the ranks of go-kart drivers."

"Any gossip to report?"

"No, Tommy, house rules. We agreed no shop talk which might prejudice Louise's position."

"Okay, I understand. How is your Out and About column going?"

"Just trivia, I am afraid. The latest is some residents over on Glover street, complaining about bad smells in the area when the wind is in a certain direction. The council inspectors have been there to check and found nothing. Apart from a few school athletics results, and a car accident at the supermarket, it has been very quiet."

"Okay Barry, the other thing I have found out is that the drug for sale in Kings is of a very high grade, compared to the widely available amateur bake. The indication is that a very clever chemist is at work. It is obvious it couldn't be a local pharmacist, because that's the first place the police would look. They must already know about the quality issue from their analysis. I still feel the link in all these matters lies somewhere in Kings U3A. The question is where?"

"You mean he is hiding in plain sight?"

"Most likely, Barry, most likely."

"Does U3A have a group who meet to discuss modern technology or the sciences?"

"Good God, yes we do, why didn't I think of that?"

Barry smiled, "there you go then, hiding in plain sight."

That evening, Tommy asked Mrs O if she knew the group convenor for U3A. He explained that he was considering joining the science and technology group, but he wasn't sure if it might be too high tech for him. Mrs O said that she knew the woman on the committee who oversaw all the groups, and would speak to her about it.

Tommy wondered how many of his thirty-two suspects might be members of the science and technology group. He didn't have to wait long. The following evening Mrs O gave him a list of seven names of U3A members who belonged. There were four men and three women. Mrs O explained they were mostly retired university people or tech hobbyists. She felt that Tommy would easily fit in.

After coffee, he retired to his room and began adding a few notes in a small notebook that he kept in his pocket.

Chapter Thirty-four

Guy Clapham was poring over the spreadsheet that Marion Steinmeyer had left him when after seven weeks assisting with the investigation, she had been recalled to the United States.

Despite the concentrated efforts of the investigative team, very little real progress had been made in finding the killer. With the absence of any weapons or DNA samples at any of the murder scenes, the killer's profile remained very vague.

Steinmeyer had admitted that the case was one of the most difficult in which she had become involved.

Clapham was left with nothing that could be corroborated, except that Kings U3A seemed to be the link. Maybe the killer was left-handed, maybe involved in the P trade, maybe a member of U3A, maybe a martial arts specialist, maybe a man or a woman, maybe already in jail? His head was spinning, but he remained dedicated to the task.

He was now reporting to Assistant Police Commissioner Rossiter twice a week, and meeting daily with the full team of twenty detectives still working on the case.

Even if Steinmeyer had not been able to establish a clear profile of the killer, she had made some general observations which Clapham had thought about. She had said that when he was ultimately identified, it would likely be found that he had a pre-disposition for violence going back to his childhood. Another trait she described was that serial killers, in her experience, were able not only to conceptualise the killing, but also to revel in the anticipation before carrying it out.

Clapham shook his head. How could a maniac carry on a normal life, maybe right here in the middle of Kings, and avoid suspicion? It was now well over two months since the last killing, so maybe he had achieved his objective? It could have been some tangled web of revenge which might never be understood.

He was jolted out of his mental review by one of his team.

"Sorry to break your train of thought boss, but we have had a report of a violent death. A woman in her shop."

Clapham jumped up. "Oh shit, I thought it was all over. Where is it?"

"Right here in Kings, only three or four miles away."

"Let's go," said Clapham, checking his pistol.

The scene should have been idyllic. A little corner florist shop full of colour and mixed scents. But it wasn't. Beyond the cordon, Clapham saw the body of a woman sprawled across the floor beside the wrapping table. At a glance, he could see by the unnatural angle of her head that the killer had struck again.

"Who found her?"

"That lady over there", replied his assistant, pointing to a woman sitting in a police car with a female officer.

The police doctor arrived, accompanied by Dr Rule the pathologist.

"Hello, Clapham, we were at a meeting together when the news came, so we thought it would save time if we came together," said Rule.

"Well gentlemen, at a rough guess, I'd say the bastard has been at work again, but I'd like your confirmation."

The medical team approached the body having dressed in the regulation blue sterile clothing which had become mandatory when investigating violent crimes.

Clapham took the chance to speak to the woman who found the body. Between sobs, she explained that she worked in the book store at the other end of the block from the florist, and had popped in on the way home to get some flowers to take to a friend in hospital later that evening.

"Poor Angela," she said. "Who would do such a thing, and during the day? She has had her little shop for as long as I can remember, everybody loves her."

"Would you mind going down to the station with this officer?" he asked, nodding towards the officer in the car, "and giving us a statement, Ms…?"

"My name is Elaine Russell, and I work part-time for Mr Cook, who owns the shop."

Clapham returned to the shop to find Barry Smart standing just outside the cordon.

"Any statement for the press, detective? Has the killer struck again? Should the town be in lockdown?"

Clapham glared at the reporter. "You know the drill, Smart. Mr Rossiter will make a statement later today. I have nothing to say."

"Is the body that of Mrs Angela Kirk, the business owner?" Barry wasn't finished, but Clapham was, and walked into the shop.

Dr Rule stepped back from the body and turned towards him.

"You're right, my friend. Our man is back at work, no doubt about it. One big hit to the throat, and a broken neck, apparently just to make sure. Ruthless bastard, isn't he?"

The scent of fresh flowers continued to pervade the area.

Clapham stepped past the cordon of yellow tape and walked along the block of shops towards the corner, glancing at each one. The last shop, with the name Collectibles emblazoned across the window in gold leaf, had a SHUT notice on a piece of string hanging in the glass door.

Clapham sharply rapped on the door. There was no reply, so he rapped again.

This time he heard steps approaching, and the door bolt slid back. The man's face was flushed, and he looked agitated.

"What's the matter with you? Can't you see the bloody shop is closed, so piss off!" Cook began to close the door, but Clapham's shoe was already in the gap. He held up his police badge.

"I am Detective Clapham of Kings police, and I want to speak to you, now, so open the door."

"Okay," said Cook, "but if it is about Mrs Kirk, I can't help you. She was a month behind with the rent. Who is going to pay that?"

Clapham could not believe his ears. A woman is murdered a few yards away, and this creep is worrying about the rent?

"We are trying to establish the time of the attack, and your name is?"

"Cook, Sam Cook. Elaine left about four o'clock. She said she was going to get some flowers for a sick friend. Next thing I hear is a woman screaming, and people rushing about saying that someone had been attacked. You people arrived, so I closed the shop. That's all."

"How did you know it was Mrs Kirk?" said Clapham.

"Someone said so."

"What about the two shops between you and the florists. Do you also own those?"

"Yes, the first one is untenanted at the moment, and the picture framer in the next one has been there for five years."

"Alright, Mr Cook, that's all for the moment, but I would like you to come down to the station tomorrow and make a statement about what you heard, and the approximate time that you heard it."

"Who did it? A domestic row I suppose. Happens all the time."

"Thank you for your co-operation," said Clapham. As he slowly walked back towards the florist shop he wondered about Cook's comments and their cold detachment from reality.

On the opposite corner, Tommy Tomlinson was looking in the window of a menswear store and watching the reflection as the man who had knocked so loudly on the closed door of Collectibles retraced his steps towards the florist. Tommy knew a policeman when he saw one.

Barry's call had alerted him to the incident, and immediately assuming that the serial killer was responsible, he was keen to observe all the surrounding activity, in case he could make any connection. It was late afternoon, so he had closed his office a little early.

At seven p.m., as he was sitting down to dinner with Mrs O, he got a text message from Barry suggesting a meeting at a local pub. With dinner over, he excused himself and rang Barry.

"What's up?"

"Hi Tommy, guess what? Mrs Kirk, the woman murdered today, was the same woman I told you about, the one who had been complaining about bad smells in her area."

They agreed to meet half an hour later.

The pub was noisy, with a local band entertaining. Barry ordered a lager, and Tommy a gin and tonic. They moved to a corner as far away from the band as possible.

Tommy asked the first question.

"Where did you find out about the poor florist lady complaining that there were bad odours in her neighbourhood?"

"The usual place for local affairs," said Barry, "the Kings council branch depot. I drop in there every week to hear the gossip. It's usually village trivia, but the locals like it. The drainage inspector told me about it, because it was puzzling him. The florist had said that it was a strong chemical smell unlike anything she had smelled before, and that it was only detectable late in the evening. She was certain that it was not a methane type smell like you would normally associate with a sewage leak. The point is that there are no commercial activities anywhere near that area anyway."

"No Barry, the point is, she said that it was only evident at night. Strange, very strange."

Chapter Thirty-five

The members of Kings U3A were clinging to each other for support, now that yet another member had been killed for no apparent reason. The florist, Angela Kirk, had been a member of the group for many years, and was convenor for the practice of *ikebana*, where she was an acknowledged expert. Her funeral was well attended, and at the request of the committee there was a strong police presence.

Tommy was there with Mrs O, who like many of the mourners, kept glancing about, trying to identify whether or not there were any strangers in the church.

Clapham was also there, carefully surveying the scene.

In his opening remarks, the priest commented on the frustration and ongoing apprehension of the local residents, and prayed for an early arrest.

"Amen," Clapham whispered to himself.

After the service Barry took Tommy aside.

"I have some interesting news Tommy. Louise said that the forensic team had found traces of P on Angela Kirk's clothing. I didn't ask her for any info because of our agreement, but she thought it might be helpful because I told you you were taking a closer interest in the case."

"I wish you hadn't told her that Barry, but let's be careful. We don't want Louise to get more involved than she would be in her day to day role as a policewoman."

"Right Tommy, sorry, but surely the florist wasn't a P user?"

"You never know these days. What surprises me is that with P being a likely link, and possibly at the centre of all this, I seem to be unable to find out where a user buys the stuff. If our killer is a supplier, then he is a real will o' the wisp, to use an old phrase. On the other hand he may be getting too sure of himself, killing the florist in broad daylight. Surely someone saw something that day?"

Tommy had forgotten that Mrs O was standing waiting, and his exchange with Barry quickly ended.

Clapham also had a puzzle. How could Angela Kirk, a well-loved member of the community, be involved with P? He decided that the only possible conclusion was that the killer must have had traces of the drug on his clothing when he struck the woman, which meant that he had been in contact with it either as a user or as a cook. Either way, it seemed to Clapham that he was now getting careless in the way he was handling his product. He noted that in Elaine Russell's statement, she said that a man had come to Collectibles after Cook had broken his hip, asking for 'stuff.' She'd had no idea what the man was talking about, and when he became very aggressive, she ran to Angela Kirk's shop, and called the police. The 111 log for that day verified her call. The man had disappeared by the time the patrol arrived. He dismissed the incident as a misunderstanding.

Back at headquarters, he stood staring at the whiteboard dominating the back wall of the operations centre. Photographs of the victims were taped by the crime scenes. Dates and times were noted. The only common denominators were that they had all been murdered in the precincts of Kings. With the exception of Jean Adams who had been strangled, probably by Christopher Luzzo, all appeared to have been victims of the killer's modus operandi, a single blow to the throat area, and all were members of U3A.

He returned to his desk and began to review the witness statements associated with each killing. He began with the early notes on the Kirk killing. He read about her recent complaint to the council about an unpleasant chemical odour in the area at night. Had she been punished for bringing nosey council inspectors into the area? It was a possibility. Next he turned to the statement that Sam Cook, the owner of the Collectibles shop, had made on the morning after the event. He had repeated the information that he had previously given to Clapham: 'Shortly after Elaine Russell had left the shop to visit a friend in hospital, he had heard a scream, and joined others at the florist shop a couple of minutes later. Ms Russell was being comforted on the pavement outside the shop, and other passers-by were peering in the doorway. Several minutes later a police car arrived, and two policemen went into the shop, asking everyone to stay outside. Someone said that the Kirk woman had been attacked. There was nothing that I could do, so I went back and closed the shop for the rest of the day.'

Clapham remembered Cook's aggressive attitude that day, but the man had said that the florist had been attacked. He did not say that she had been killed, but he didn't ask if she was all right. Clapham decided the man was a callous bastard, but that was not a crime. He knew some of his colleagues were of the same ilk. He picked up the next file.

The following afternoon Tommy decided to return to the scene of the Kirk killing. He had noted the loud exchange between the owner of the Collectibles and the policeman. First, he went into the shop next to the florist. It was small and messy, with a strong smell of varnish. A wide variety of photo frames adorned the walls. A large white painted bin held a selection of what claimed to be limited edition prints. Tommy could tell at a glance that they were machine printed, and only limited in number by the amount of paper fed into a printing machine, probably somewhere in China.

A middle-aged man came from the rear of the shop.

"Gidday, how can I help?" he said, rubbing his hands on a piece of tattered towelling. "Something to be framed?" he hopefully continued.

"Not today," said Tommy, "I'm just looking around the area for the insurance company. We heard that there have been complaints about chemical fumes in the area. Maybe a fire hazard you know, these older two storey timber buildings would go off like roman candles in case of a fire."

"Well whatever it is mate, it is not coming from here. A small pot of varnish goes a long way in my trade."

"I'm sure it does," said Tommy. "So you haven't noticed anything yourself? You are probably so used to using varnish, the smell doesn't register with you."

"Can't say that I have noticed anything, although poor Angela next door did mention something about bad smells at night, but then she lived above the shop. I get away home about six. I use upstairs for a bit of storage and varnish fumes could tend to linger, I suppose."

"What about the gentleman at the end shop?"

"That's bloody Sam Cook, and he is no gentleman. Owns all these shops. Never speaks to anyone, yet he has all these weirdos coming to his stupid shop. Funny people who collect stamps and old books, they say. I direct credit my rent, so I never see him. His lovely wife went to South Africa and never came back. I wasn't surprised. You heard about the killing?"

"Yes, I read about it in the papers. Terrible business, and terrible for you, right next door, and in broad daylight, I understand."

"The police have been good. I gave them a statement. I'm usually in my workshop, and if a customer comes in I hear the bell. What reason could anyone have to kill poor Angela? Couldn't have been money, and I gather nothing was stolen. I keep a police issue baton by the counter, but who would want to rob a picture framer?"

Tommy wished the man well and left. He walked right around the block, noting that a high brick wall obscured the rear of the shops. Each property had a stoutly reinforced door to the street, an essential precaution to deter burglars, thought Tommy. He reached his car, and took out his notebook.

Alongside the list of names he had got from Mrs O, he put a question mark alongside that of Sam Cook.

Chapter Thirty-six

Sam Cook was frustrated, and when he was in this frame of mind, he always asked Amelia for her advice.

"Amelia dear, what was I to do? The stupid Kirk woman brought it on herself, running to the council, getting health inspectors involved. Why can't people mind their own business? My regulars are wary of the police around the place, and so my business is suffering. Now I have to find a new tenant. That's the part I hate, finding a new neighbour who can keep to themselves. This time it will be the shop only. I am not having anyone living on my block at night again."

The chat with his wife made him feel better, so he stood up from the tin trunk where he had been sitting and walked to his workbench. Various containers of chemicals lined the shelves to the side. He began preparing to produce another batch of P. Not too much, about twenty-five thousand pounds worth. This would keep the market supplied for about two weeks on average.

His two main distributors outside of the Kings area were getting impatient, but they had kept the market alive while he had sojourned in Italy. With the increased police activity in the area, he had decided to hand over the larger amounts of the drug in a supermarket carpark some distance away.

For the dozen or so local addicts, he continued to supply them in his office during working hours.

Some were genuine book or stamp collectors, so they provided a screen of legitimacy, which was cover for their regular visits.

Later that evening, his production finished, he sampled the drug in the same small quantity as usual, and then settled down staring at the wall that he had devoted to exhibiting all the newspaper clippings about the Kings killings. He smiled with satisfaction at the developing fear which had grown over the period, and the stupidity of the police who were unable to find any clues, anywhere.

The latest clippings from the *Kings Herald* were using more and more extravagant language in their descriptions of the killer. He was at once deranged, sadistic, wicked, insane, and even feral, according to the reporter.

Sam thought Amelia had said something, but it was muffled. He was happy that she was still interested in his exploits.

Too sleepy to go to his bedroom, he decided to sleep on the canvas bed he kept in the corner of the cellar. He turned off the exhaust system, satisfied that there were no lingering fumes.

Sitting in his car opposite the back gate to Collectibles, the ex-naval officer with an ear for vibrations and mechanical sounds noticed that the steady hum, which he had identified as coming from somewhere in the rear of the block of shops, had stopped. Tommy had noticed a very slight chemical odour for a moment or two when he had arrived, but thought it might have come from a passing diesel bus.

He decided to drive a little further, and park more downwind from the shops. He was just about to start off when a large dark sedan stopped right behind him. In the dim light, Tommy thought it was a Volvo. A man stepped out, and walking towards him, shone a torch through the open window.

"Good evening sir. A bit late to be stopped in such a quiet place. I am Guy Clapham, with Kings police, here is my identification," he said, shining the torch on the plastic card in his hand. "Can I see your driver's licence?"

Tommy reached for his wallet and handed over his licence.

"Mr Tomlinson, have you been drinking tonight?"

"No officer," said Tommy, "I was on my way home and felt a bit dizzy, so I stopped for a moment. I am okay now, must have been working too hard."

"Are you at the same address, Mr Tomlinson."

"Yes, I am renting a room from Mrs Osborne at Pine Street."

"Would that be Mrs Lynda Osborne?"

"Yes indeed, a very nice lady, why?"

"I knew her first husband, Roger Osborne. Not a very nice man, sir. Here you are," he said, handing Tommy back his licence. "I suggest you drive home slowly, and get checked by a doctor tomorrow if you are still not well."

Tommy started his Audi and drove quietly off, cursing himself for being so stupid as to park so close to Collectibles. It then occurred to him that he might not be the only person interested in that particular area of town at night. Did the police know something? Why was Clapham, the lead detective in the investigation, in the area?

The next meeting of the U3A Science and Technology group was to take place at the home of a member, because as there were only eight in the group, the host for the month could provide the morning tea without too much effort.

Tommy had been accepted into the group and arrived a few minutes before ten in the morning, at the address given in the email he had received along with the agenda for the meeting.

He was welcomed into the home of Tim O'Connor, the convenor of the group. O'Connor was a retired university professor with a degree in electronics, a fact that he never failed to mention.

When all the members had arrived, he started the meeting and introduced Tommy to the others.

There were handshakes all round, and then O'Connor asked Tommy to say something about himself and his interests for the benefit of the group.

Tommy explained that he had a naval background, without being too specific, and was now a consultant to a marine insurance broker specialising in claim adjustments. He had a small coin collection as a hobby. "Nothing special," he emphasised.

Sitting down, he found himself directly opposite Sam Cook, who looked across at him.

"I have a few old coins in my shop, Tommy. Drop by some time, you might be interested."

"Thanks," said Tommy, "I will." Cook's face was expressionless, and his brooding deep-set eyes made Tommy uneasy.

The member whose turn it was to give a talk, began to explain the intricacies involved in the design of robots. Tommy was fascinated by the man's depth of knowledge, and remembered Mrs O's remark to him when she was describing the membership of U3A. She said that 'everyone used to be someone.'

Tommy decided it would be a good time to find out who or what Sam Cook 'used to be'.

Chapter Thirty-seven

The usual monthly meeting of U3A had been delayed as a mark of respect for Morris Kincaid, the late president. His funeral had been attended by national figures, including the Minister of Police. With the death of Ms Kirk, the florist, the mood of the town, and especially the U3A membership, had moved from one of underlying panic to one of frantic speculation, continuing to be fuelled by gossip and innuendo. Clapham had almost given up distributing follow-up instructions to his staff because of the deluge of unsubstantiated information being passed on to the inquiry team. DC Rossiter had unofficially described the situation to the Police Commissioner as 'moving towards chaos'.

The reprimand he received for the comment was still ringing in his ears as he stood on the stage before an audience which filled the hall to overflowing. For the fourth time in three months, he stared out at a group of residents eager for information, but with little hope of delivering to them anything substantive. He took a deep breath and began to speak.

"Members of the Kings community, I want to begin by thanking you all, once again, for the patience you have shown during the investigation, and the ongoing support given to the police..."

He was interrupted by a voice from the back of the hall.

"Yes, all very good, but are you any nearer to catching the bastard? Bullshit is getting us nowhere."

The man was a stranger to U3A members, but they assumed that he was a resident. They were wrong. Clapham recognised him as a reporter for a national newspaper who had been hanging around the area for more than a week looking for a story.

DC Rossiter stared in the direction of the man and continued. "Yes sir, to answer your question, we believe that we are much closer to finding the killer. We have had the benefit of a visit from an American expert in criminal profiling, and that process has helped us to eliminate a large percentage of the local population."

Rossiter went on to reiterate that constant police patrols were to continue, with a number of unmarked cars operating.

Ron Barber, who was acting as the President of Kings U3A following the death of Morris Kincaid, thanked the policeman, and reminded those present to continue to be vigilant and security-conscious. The meeting then followed the usual agenda, with convenors reporting on the month's activities, as everyone tried to retain a business as usual attitude, despite the dark cloud hanging over the community.

Sam Cook had been in Italy when the announcement of the arrival of Marion Steinmeyer from the FBI had been in the news, and this was the first he had heard about it. He didn't like surprises, because he saw himself as the one who controlled events, not the stupid police. Alarm set in, and first his left leg began to twitch, then his right arm, as he suddenly became nervous and confused.

Nobody noticed when a member of the audience quietly slipped out a side door before the end of the meeting.

To allay his panic, Cook did what he always did when under pressure. He started chopping his left hand into the open palm of his right hand as he hurried to his car. A flood of questions began to present themselves. What profile did they have? What was his profile? The bloody police always knew more than they revealed. To calm himself, he dipped into the emergency supply of P that he kept in his jacket pocket and quickly swallowed two tablets. His usual fix was one, but he decided that this was an emergency.

Arriving back at Collectibles, he told Elaine Russell that he was closing the shop as some urgent business had come up, and he would let her know when he wanted her back, indicating that it 'might be a few days.'

Chapter Thirty-eight

Following the U3A meeting, Tommy decided it was time to have a talk with Barry to explain the plan of action he had in mind. He had received a call from his old colleague Mark James, who wanted to know if he was making any progress in the recovery of the missing stamp collection.

They met at the coffee shop that had become so popular in the early days of the investigations.

Tommy began by talking about Cook and his brooding character.

Barry agreed, commenting, "one or two people have noticed that he is even more bad tempered than before he had his fall. But it doesn't seem to deter the regular customers who visit his shop. Mrs Russell told me that on the odd occasion that she opened the shop for an hour or two while Cook was away, several regulars cursed the fact he had been away so long."

Tommy explained that at the last U3A meeting of the Science and Technology group, Cook had invited him to come to Collectibles to peruse a collection of old coins.

"While I am there, I will keep my eye open for any offering of stamps that may be on display. Have you heard anything on the grapevine?"

"Nothing at all, Tommy. Everyone is too focused on finding the killer. I know I am. An exclusive break would make my career. There is one thing though," said Barry.

"Well, out with it."

Barry looked furtively around the café, then whispered, "It's something that Louise noticed before she was transferred. Clapham had asked her to check old records in the station to see if she could find any convictions relating to residents in the past. Guess what? She found a charge of assault against Cook, which was withdrawn through lack of evidence. As it had happened almost thirty years ago, Clapham dismissed it as irrelevant to the present case when she told him, and no action was taken. The complainant was a customer of Cook's father, who claimed he had been cheated out of several valuable stamps he had left at the shop for appraisal. Cook jnr., as he was then, went to the man's house, where allegedly a scuffle took place. Cook struck out at the man with his fist, catching him a glancing blow and smashing out the reinforced glass centre panel of his front door. Two days later the man withdrew the charge."

"Good God, man," exclaimed Tommy, "Sam Cook smashed in someone's front door with his bare hands? Must have scared the crap out of the customer, so much so that he withdrew the charge."

"Old habits die hard, Barry. Louise may have unwittingly found our killer hiding in plain sight. I will not be surprised to find that Cook is left-handed. I'll go to the shop tomorrow to look at his coins. Don't tell Louise yet that you have passed on her news to me."

Chapter Thirty-nine

Tommy rang Collectibles to see if Cook was there.

"Hello there Sam, it's Tommy Tomlinson from U3A. You mentioned you had some coins that you thought I might be interested in."

"You're the ex-navy man?" said Cook.

"Yes, that's me."

"Well I'm shut, because I'm being pestered. But if you come along this afternoon after 2 o'clock, I'll let you in for a few minutes."

"Thank you, Sam. After 2 o'clock then."

Tommy put the phone down. How strange, he thought. Who described themselves as being pestered?

He parked his car opposite Collectibles twenty minutes before the agreed time. The door to the shop was closed. He checked the Glock in his shoulder holster was on safety, and was about to get out of the car when a man approached the shop from the florist end and knocked on the door.

Cook must have been expecting him because the door was quickly opened and closed as the man stepped inside.

Less than three minutes later the door opened again, the same man came out, and scurried around the corner of Collectibles, disappearing from sight.

Was he delivering something or collecting, Tommy wondered.

A few minutes after two, Tommy knocked on Cook's door.

When it opened he was shocked to see that Cook was wearing pyjamas with a long heavy coat over the top. His feet were bare, and his hair dishevelled. The shoulders of the coat were coated in a dusting of white powder and a pervasive pungent chemical odour hung in the air.

"Come on then, come in. It's bloody freezing," he said. Tommy had just checked the thermometer in his car, and it was reading 24 degrees.

"Sam, if you're not well, I can come another time."

"Who said I'm not well? Are they talking about me again? I won't let them into the shop you know. Kincaid was here last night, but I got rid of him. No more trouble there," he laughed. "I know they are all trying to haunt me. Losers, the lot of them. Amelia was right."

Tommy quickly made his decision.

"Sam, I've left my glasses in the car. I'll just slip back and get them," he said turning to the door, his hand on the Glock.

"You're one of them, aren't you, you bastard. Kincaid and that bloody Luzzo have sent you, haven't they?" He started towards Tommy, left hand raised, but tripped slightly on the edge of the long coat he was wearing, giving Tommy just enough time to reach the door. He slammed it shut behind him and made for his car.

His heart racing from the confrontation, he got in and locked his doors. Cook was insane. Something had released the demons in an already demented mind. The monster had now come out of hiding.

As Tommy raced off to the police station, there was no movement at Collectibles.

Chapter Forty

It had been a quiet afternoon at the Kings police station, but that all changed when Tommy Tomlinson arrived asking to see Guy Clapham urgently.

He was soon seated in front of the tired detective who for a moment had difficulty in processing the burst of information being delivered by Tommy.

"You're saying that Sam Cook is the killer?"

"I'm certain of it," said Tommy. "The man's insane. I was making a business call to his shop and found him completely dishevelled and covered in a white dust, which I took to be some kind of drug. You could smell it in the air. You have to act before he kills again."

Clapham had heard enough. He called together the members of his squad and five minutes later, two unmarked cars were racing to Collectibles. Tommy followed at a safe distance.

They could see smoke some distance off, and heard the fire trucks being dispatched on the emergency channel which was open in both cars. As Clapham and his squad arrived, half a dozen onlookers were already standing in the street looking at the flames which were beginning to roar out of one of the upstairs windows of Collectibles. A red glow was visible through the glass front window, contrasting with the gold lettering which spelt out the name of the old shop. A steady breeze was blowing the smoke high into the air.

As they approached the shop there was the muffled roar of an explosion, and suddenly flames shot out of the roof of the adjoining building. The dry sixty-year-old timber construction of the block was now fuelling the flames, sending them more than twenty metres into the air.

"Bloody hell," yelled Clapham, "everyone get back, there may be more explosions!"

Two fire trucks arrived and the ten crew members started running out hoses.

Clapham ran to the chief fire officer. "Good to see you."

"Do we know if there is anyone in there, Guy?"

"The shop's shut, but we think there is a man in there who may be our killer. Also, a witness has said there are strong chemicals in there."

"I would say he's right, mate. My guess is that we have a P lab on fire here," said the fireman. "The smell and the explosions are typical, in my experience. My team are not going to attempt going in, but we'll do our best to contain it. We will have to set up a decontamination spray unit to deal with any possible chemical problems."

Just at that moment the front window of the shop shattered, and a ball of flame rolled up the side of the building, showering embers everywhere. The fire quickly spread to the framer's shop.

Nearly fifteen minutes had passed since the first alarm had been given, and now the whole block was in danger of being consumed in an uncontrollable firestorm as the breeze picked up.

Tommy stood back in awe, and was soon joined by Barry Smart, his eyes wide with excitement.

"Here is your big story Barry", he said. "Cook is undoubtedly the killer. He tried to attack me with a left-handed karate chop when I visited the store only forty-five minutes ago. He was as high as a kite, covered in white powder." Tommy had already decided that the white powder was P.

The crowd of spectators was swelling by the minute, and soon the rumour spread that the Kings serial killer was trapped inside the building. Everyone was holding up a phone to capture a picture of the disaster.

"Don't waste your time boys," a man shouted at the firemen struggling with the high pressure hoses. "Let the bastard burn."

The additional policemen now arriving were busy trying to maintain public safety.

A gasp went up when the biggest explosion yet burst through the roof of almost the entire block. Portions of the building were now collapsing inwards. The structure was doomed.

In the confusion, and because of the crowd's morbid curiosity in the event, the haggard man wearing a long dusty coat over an old pair of jeans and with a black beanie covering his white hair went unnoticed as he walked towards the black Lexus parked in a side street. He was speaking aloud, as if to a companion.

"I'm sorry I had to leave you like this Amelia, but I know you will have felt no pain. You shouldn't worry about me, I will be occupied with unfinished business."

He opened the door of his car, smiled at his reflection in the mirror, and drove quietly away.

Chapter Forty-one

He had known for a long time that because of his business activity, he would one day need a bolt hole and another identity. This was that day, and just as he had planned, the small cottage in an adjoining suburb well away from Kings was fully equipped to provide for all of his needs for the foreseeable future.

Opening the garage door, he started the Honda Accord and backed it out to the driveway, leaving room for the Lexus to be driven in and the door closed. Henry Charlton, aka Samuel Cook, was shown in the local electoral roll as the owner of number forty-six Langton Drive, Southside. His profession was given as engineer.

It was more than twenty-four hours before any forensic examination of what was left of Collectibles could begin, as the entire block of shops had been consumed. Wisps of smoke were still emanating from the charred layers of books as a team of specialists from the central fire department began their work. Alongside them was a team from the police serious crime unit. Together, clad in their yellow hazmat suits, they resembled a gathering of space travellers. A faint chemical odour still hung in the air, proving their need for protection from toxic substances.

The whole area had been blocked off and guarded throughout the night as hundreds of local residents came to the site, hoping for news that the Kings killer had perished in the blaze.

At nine a.m. DC Rossiter, Clapham by his side, read a prepared statement to the assembled media circus which had descended on Kings. In it, he asked for patience as the site was being examined by experts. The whereabouts of the owner, Mr Samuel Cook, was unknown, but he was wanted for questioning, and anyone with information about the incident should call Crimestoppers or their local police station. He refused to take questions, stating that a further media briefing would be held as soon as new information came to hand.

Late in the afternoon, the site examination reached the cellar of the building where Collectibles had stood. A small hydraulic excavator was removing debris under the watchful eye of a senior fire officer, when the driver called to him.

"There is a large metal chest or box just under the leading edge of the bucket. Do you want to check it before I lever it out?"

"Let me look first," said the officer.

He carefully picked his way into the debris. The top of the chest and two sides had been revealed, blackened and covered in soot. Stooping down, he struck off the small padlock with the end of his fire axe and lifted the lid.

"Ooh shit!" he exclaimed, reeling backwards from the horror staring out at him from within the chest. It was the half-mummified body of a woman, her eyes glazed over, but locked in a hideous stare.

"Good God." He pushed the talk button on his radio.

"Get the forensic team down here. We have what is left of a body."

Prompted by curiosity, the excavator driver climbed down from the cab and joined the fireman.

Unprepared for the sight which met him, he violently retched, and white with shock, slowly returned to his seat.

Two minutes later, he rang his wife.

"Andrea, it's me. I'm at the Collectibles fire. I just uncovered a tin trunk with a woman's body in it." He was breathless. "I said a tin box with a woman's body in it. No, I don't know who it is, how could I, for Christ's sake! The police are all over it. No, that's all, I'll see you tonight." He put down his phone, and watched as the members of the forensic team gathered around the box.

With some difficulty, they removed the remaining debris and freed it. Three men were then able to lift it and carefully carry it up to a police van.

Five minutes later, the excavator driver's wife put down her phone after speaking to her sister about her husband's call.

One hour later, a rumour that the body of Sam Cook's wife had been found in the ruins of Collectibles had circulated around most of Kings inhabitants.

Lynda Osbourne had spoken to Elaine Russell, who said she had never believed Cook's story about his wife going to Africa and divorcing him from there. Obviously, the brute had murdered the poor woman and buried the body in the shop. She had always felt there was something funny going on there.

Chapter Forty-two

The reports from the forensic pathologist, the fire investigation specialists, the police serious incident team, the central DNA database, and the drug squad, took almost three months to complete.

DC Rossiter aged almost overnight under the pressure being brought to bear by not only the Minister of Police, but also by politicians of all hues. The situation had not been helped by the constant attention of the media. One or two of the competing channels had even employed psychics to deliver their sometimes very odd assessments of the case.

Guy Clapham was now part of a team of twelve senior detectives who had been seconded to Kings from all over the county, depending on their particular area of expertise. There were an additional ten detectives and detective sergeants working on the case, rostered twenty-four seven.

The lives of the citizens of the Kings community had, during this period of hiatus, almost returned to their normal patterns. There had been no more incidents to cause alarm. The alleged killer had disappeared on the day of the fire, and despite a complete lack of evidence, many had decided his body had been totally consumed by the fire. That his wife's body had been identified through dental records brought to a close what had been a rich source of gossip since she had allegedly departed for South Africa, years before.

The funeral of Amelia Cook was well-attended by the members of U3A out of a sense of community, because nobody had come forward to claim her body. The group met all the expenses, and the local funeral home had waived any additional charges.

The manhunt for Samuel Cook went nationwide, with a reward set at 100,000 pounds for information leading to his arrest. The photograph accompanying the notice was from the U3A archive, and was unfortunately from his younger days. His hair was dark and brushed straight back, but it was his hooded black eyes staring straight into the camera that evinced the image of a man with a dark and threatening nature.

Tommy Tomlinson complained to Guy Chapman that the image was nothing like the man who had confronted him on the day of the fire. Chapman said it was the best they could do at the time.

An odd fact was that a black Lexus sedan registered in the name of Samuel Cook was nowhere to be found. The bank account for Collectibles was showing a credit balance of twenty-one pounds and an account in the name of S.C Cook was also in credit for seven pounds. A deposit account for seventy-five thousand pounds had been withdrawn in cash on the day of the fire. There had been no use of a credit card in the name of S.C. Cook since.

Both Rossiter and Chapman wanted to believe that the man really had gone up in smoke, but until they had conclusive evidence of that, the search would go on.

Chapter Forty-three

The man living at number forty-six Langton Drive in the suburb of Southside was happy. The gay owner of the uni-sex salon in the mall had totally understood why the middle-aged man had come into the salon weeks before for a makeover. His white hair was short and in the past had been inexpertly cut. He had cut it himself, on the night of the fire, when his rage had been replaced with pragmatism.

He had explained that there was a new woman in his life, so a good cut, together with a light brown tint, would take years off his age. Henry Charlton had left the salon a new man. Lightly tinted glasses with neutral lenses completed the transformation. He was, however, quite nonplussed by the suggestion made by the barber, as he was leaving, 'that maybe they could meet for coffee some time'. How dare this stranger interfere in my private life, he thought. Why did everyone hound him?

Parking the Honda on the street, he entered his new home. Now he would avenge all those who had been so cruel to Sam Cook. Oh yes, he thought, he had been patient enough. Now was the time to let those in Kings who thought they were safe, think again.

At Goh Coffee, Tommy and Barry had their regular meeting.

"Nothing new then, Tommy?"

"Nothing to report Barry, I'm sorry."

They both stared into their coffees.

They had met at least a dozen times in the last three months, always with the same outcome.

Nothing.

"Barry, one thing I do know, or at least believe, is that the killer always returns to the scene of the crime. If he is still alive, he'll be back. He's nuts!"

"What about the stamps?" said Barry. "If he's alive, as you think, then the stamps are either with him or under his control, maybe stashed somewhere?"

"I agree. With any luck, our killer may also be a classic hoarder. His bloody shop had the signs of a hoarder, books everywhere, in no particular order. But that doesn't advance our cause. There must be some little clue, somewhere, that is being overlooked either by the police or by us. But the worrying thing is, with time passing, our chances of discovering it are rapidly receding."

"What about his Lexus?"

"Good point, Barry, but it will be locked away in a warehouse or lockup somewhere, waiting to be discovered in twenty years' time. Cook is not just mad, but he is extremely devious with it."

"Okay then. What about his P manufacturing, and his clients? He wouldn't give up his business that easily, would he?"

"No, I think not, but maybe he has simply moved to another area. The drug squad, from what I hear, have picked up all the known addicts around the place, but nobody is talking. The police think that the drought caused by Cook's disappearance has simply resulted in another supplier moving in. By the way Barry, Mark James my old insurance mate is still in the game with us. He thinks that with us on the ground, he has just as good a chance of a recovery as going through the hassle of hiring a local investigator."

The two men agreed to meet again at the end of the week.

It was just by chance that Constable Louise Banks was assisting the duty sergeant on the front desk of her police station when a young and attractive Italian woman walked in.

The sergeant sprang into life. Louise had never seen him smile until now.

"Yes Miss, how can we help?"

Her voice was cultured, with very little accent. Her English, perfect.

"I am hoping that you can help me. I am looking for a Mr Samuel Cook. He was in Italy some months ago. I escorted him for a while, when he was recovering from a bad fall. My father is the concierge at the hotel where he stayed. I am here on holiday, and would like to see him again. All we had was his passport number from when he checked in. Fortunately, my father had kept a note from a package that he had delivered. It gave Kings as the return address, but no street."

The sergeant began to speak. "Miss, I have some bad... ow!" Louise, smiling, had just kicked him in the ankle.

"What the sergeant was about to say, Miss...?"

"My name is Violetta Cavalli, and I live in Stresa, northern Italy."

"A beautiful place," said Louise, smiling at the sergeant.

"What the sergeant was going to say, Miss Cavalli, is that although the timing is bad, because we are so busy, we may be able to help you."

"You are so kind," said Violetta.

"Sergeant, shall I show Miss Cavalli into an interview room?"

"Good idea."

As soon as Louise and the Italian visitor were out of sight, the sergeant was on the phone to the Kings inquiry centre, asking for detective Clapham.

Three minutes later Clapham raced towards the outlying station in his Volvo, blue lights flashing.

Louise was getting a cup of coffee for her visitor and thinking about the next step when the desk sergeant appeared.

"You did the right thing, Lou. I was elsewhere. Clapham is on his way here, so delay the conversation as much as you can until he arrives."

Clapham parked the Volvo next to a red Alfa Romeo with Italian registration plates. He took no notice of the two occupants wearing sunglasses.

As the sergeant escorted Clapham to the interview room, he explained again how the woman had come in asking about Samuel Cook.

Louise introduced Clapham as her colleague, and by way of explanation repeated the details of Ms Cavalli's association with Cook in Italy.

"We would like to help you Ms Cavalli, but first I have to ask you, have you heard about Mr Cook's fire, and the suspicion that he may have murdered his wife? He is a wanted man, with a reward on his head."

Violetta Cavalli seemed unperturbed.

"It is very strange. He told me that his ex-wife had left him to go to live in South Africa."

"Yes, that was the story he told locals as well, but the fact is we found Mrs Cook's body in the remains of his shop," said Clapham. "So you have heard nothing about all the accusations against him?"

"I read some gossip in a national newspaper a day or two ago. It didn't sound like the Mr Cook that I knew. I have just arrived from Italy, and we have enough crime there to keep our newspapers busy without reporting international crime."

Clapham tried the direct approach. "So you have no idea where Mr Cook may be?"

"Of course not, that is why I have come to you. You English have a big reputation like Sherlock Holmes."

"That's fiction, of course," said Clapham.

The woman smiled, and remained composed. Louise was forming the opinion that there was some reason other than a simple reunion that had brought her halfway across Europe.

Ms Cavalli stood up. "Well, thank you very much for your information. It seems like I won't be seeing Mr Cook again after all. I will tour a little, while I am here. I love the English villages, so different to Italia."

She shook hands with Louise and Clapham. Louise showed her to the door of the station.

"*Arrivederci*," she called, as she quickly walked towards the red Alfa Romeo.

Clapham was still sitting in the interview room as Louise entered.

"What the hell was all that about Louise? She didn't know about the biggest manhunt for years? Pull the other one!"

"I agree, Guy. Maybe she came here instead of Kings, so as not to draw too much attention to herself? There were two men in an Alfa waiting for her, and they didn't look like her brothers. Maybe Cook crossed them somehow, when he was in Italy. She said he had stayed in a very posh hotel in Stresa where her father was the concierge.

"Okay," said Clapham, "you are officially seconded onto my team. I'll tell your boss. You get on to the manager of the hotel whatever, and ask him if there was any incident associated with Sam Cook while he was staying there. Then speak to the police in Stresa and see if they have any comment."

Louise was excited. This was why she had joined the police. She couldn't wait to tell Barry.

As the red Alfa Romeo drove slowly towards Kings with the driver following its GPS, Violetta spoke to a man in Stresa, explaining that the police had no additional information on Cook's whereabouts they were prepared to share. She was instructed to wait another week in the hotel on the outskirts of Kings that had been arranged.

"Keep to the left Bruno, you idiot," she shouted at the driver. "I didn't come here to have an accident."

"*Scusa, signorina,*" he said.

Thirty minutes later Constable Banks had news from Italy that couldn't wait. Clapham was on the phone to DC Rossiter when she burst into the interview room. Sensing her urgency, he told Rossiter he would call him back in a moment.

"Guy, the Italian Police have just issued a warrant for the arrest of Sam Cook for the murder of a drug dealer in Stresa during his stay there. An Interpol alert was issued yesterday."

"Bloody hell," said Clapham. "That explains the visit of our Ms Cavalli. Now the Mafia want him as well. The bastard better hope that we find him before they do."

He reconnected his call to Rossiter with the news. They agreed to put a so-called 'loose watch' on the red Alfa Romeo, as soon as they could confirm its registration plate number from the CCTV at the station. They had to be careful because the Italians had not committed any crime.

When Rossiter got hold of the Interpol notice later that day, he read that Cook, the alleged murderer of the drug dealer in Stresa, had dropped a card identifying him as a member of the Kings U3A in the victim's Maserati. Also found was a piece of monogrammed notepaper identified as having come from Cook's hotel room.

Chapter Forty-four

Louise Banks, against all the rules, had told her partner about the unusual meeting with the Italian woman, and Clapham's conclusion that with the Interpol notice now live, she was somehow connected to the Mafia.

Barry was now on the lookout for a red Alfa Romeo. He didn't have to wait long, because as he sat down with Tommy for the next meeting at Goh Coffee, a red Alfa Romeo stopped outside. A very attractive young woman accompanied by two athletic-looking young men in track-suits came into the café and chose a table well away from them.

Barry put his hand to his mouth and whispered, "Do you see what I see, Tommy?"

"Just relax, and for God's sake, don't stare," said his companion. "If they have been sent by the Mafia and know where Cook is, they would not be sitting here drinking coffee, would they?"

"Right Tommy, so now what's the plan?"

"I've been thinking about clues Barry, and the standout at the moment for me is this – where is the black Lexus? I know there are stories about stolen luxury cars finding their way to Poland and the Middle East, but I don't think our man would risk it. No, it's somewhere around this area, Kings and the surrounds. It's time I visited the Lexus dealer. No doubt the police went there first, but I'll put on my insurance hat and see how far I get."

The Italians got up and left the café, quietly driving off in the Alfa.

"Those guys look nasty," said Barry. "Probably knife men. Italians like knives."

"Well, now it is a three-way race, my friend," said Tommy, "winner take all. I want those stamps, but first we have to see Cook dead and buried."

"I'm writing my story," said Barry, "but every time I think I'm getting to the end, something else happens."

"Patience, lad, patience. I'm going Lexus hunting."

Tommy's experience had taught him that insurance was a topic carefully avoided by senior executives, and usually left to the firm's accountant to deal with, along with tax returns and other official form-filling duties. This was the case at All Nippon Motors, the Lexus dealer for the area.

He gave the receptionist his card and asked to see the accountant on an insurance matter, and no, he didn't have an appointment. Two minutes later he was sitting across the desk from a nervous-looking young man who kept glancing at his computer screen as if waiting for a message from either God or his wife.

Tommy explained that he was an auditor for the insurance company as well as a claims adjuster, and had one or two questions about a Lexus belonging to Samuel Cook, the wanted man.

"Mr Cook's Lexus has been nothing but trouble, Mr Tomlinson," he said, taking a moment to read Tommy's card. "First the trouble over the cash payment. He paid in fifties and hundreds, and when I counted it out, it was three hundred pounds short. He accused me of theft, but the manager intervened to save me, because as he said later, he had taken Mr Cook off at the ankles over his trade-in, so a lousy three hundred was not worth arguing about."

"Very troubling, I'm sure," said Tommy. "So your company sold an insurance policy with the car?"

"Oh yes, the salesmen get extra commission for selling a policy, but I explained all that to the police."

"Do you by any chance have a copy of the policy handy? Sorry to trouble you, but just so I can confirm it, if someone makes a claim against it."

"The police are looking for the car, I hear," said the man. "I think it will be out of the country by now. We have had one or two Lexus models disappear without trace."

"In that case, I'm sure there will be a claim sooner or later, either by his family, if he has one, or by someone representing him."

The man went to a steel cabinet and took out a folder, giving it to Tommy.

He quickly scanned the three-page document which had the usual multiple paragraphs of exclusions. Then he noticed a smaller sheet pinned to the third page. It provided for a third party to meet the payments if the owner was absent or incapacitated. There was a name printed in the appropriate box.

Tommy showed it to the accountant.

"What's this? It doesn't look like part of the main policy," asked Tommy.

"You're right," said the man. "I found it after the police had gone, so I pinned it with the policy. I like to be tidy."

"So the police did not see it?"

"No, it's not that important is it?"

"No, I suppose not," said Tommy, "but I'll note the name, just in case, you know."

"No problem. Anything else I can help you with today Mr Tomlinson?"

Tommy thanked the man and left.

The name he had written down was Henry Charlton, but there had been no address. Tommy assumed that in the rush to complete the sale, the salesman had omitted to check the paperwork.

The name was not familiar to him, but it was not too common. Was he an old friend of Cook? He headed for the local council office to check the electoral roll.

Chapter Forty-five

The body of the local hairdresser was found by a jogger early that morning in a local park. The area had come to the attention of the police once or twice over the previous six months because of alleged drug dealing and other associated activities. But now, it was about to become infamous. It was quickly established that the man had been struck with a single blow to the throat which had smashed his larynx. His neck was broken.

The Kings serial killer had once again made his mark on the already anxious and apprehensive residents.

By the time Barry Smart reached the scene, it had been closed off with the usual police lines.

At any other time it would have been an idyllic scene, with the early daffodils and freesias blooming amongst the old oaks, which were showing green tips. The grassy surrounds had been manicured by dedicated council staff. But today, the mothers wheeling giant three-wheel prams, the dog walkers, and the strollers were all absent.

The large blue tent erected by the serious incident squad and the yellow, 'do not cross tapes' added to the now sombre atmosphere.

Clapham was early on the scene, as was the police pathologist.

The body had been posed on its back, legs together, and arms by the side. Unremarkable, except that the man's head was twisted at forty-five degrees to the body.

"Well, Doc," said the detective, "at least one mystery is solved. Cook, the miserable bastard, didn't perish in the fire."

"Yes," replied his companion, "but he has stepped outside the Kings area, and this poor soul doesn't look old enough to qualify for U3A membership. If he is changing his modus operandi, he's going to make the job even tougher than it already is. The one thing he hasn't changed is his method of killing."

Tommy had found a very co-operative clerk at the council office and established that a Mr Henry Charlton did in fact live at number forty-six Langton Drive, Southside. It had been too late on the previous afternoon to check out the address, and he decided to drive to Southside this morning. It was a distance of more than twenty miles.

He had checked his office before setting off just before ten a.m. There was an email message advising him of a special general meeting of Kings U3A, to confirm the election of a new president. It was set for two pm. that afternoon.

Once on his way, he turned on the local twenty-four hour news station, and was startled to hear that a body exhibiting all the hallmarks of the Kings serial killer had been found that morning in a park in Southside. He stopped the car and rang Barry.

Sam Cook had also received the message about the U3A meeting, forwarded by his server to the second default address that he had registered months before. He would have to hurry, but it would be worth it, he thought. He had set up an appointment with that crass hairdresser the previous evening, and had been able to satisfactorily punish him for his rudeness. He was still amused at the man's eager acceptance of the meeting, foolishly imagining that Cook was attracted to him. Now providence had given him the ideal opportunity to also punish, with one bold action, a large number of U3A members.

The twenty ten-kilo bags of ammonium nitrate had easily fitted into the Lexus. The clerk at the farm supplies store was impressed with Mr Henry Charlton's knowledge of chemicals when they had chatted about the farmlet he was developing. His two visits to the store also involved buying some other farming items. The two small drums of diesel were reserves for his small tractor, he explained to the man.

Removing the rear seats of the Lexus had been difficult, but the flat floor provided for the perfect combination of the simple ingredients required for the bomb. The solid construction of the car, with its heavily insulated floor, would help to pressurise the explosion for a milli-second, ensuring a wide spread of shrapnel. Cook had assembled the timing device and detonator from one of the many instructive diagrams available on the internet. As a young chemist, he had been fascinated by the use of a similar bomb in 1995 by Timothy McVeagh, the Oklahoma bomber, which had resulted in the deaths of 168 men women and children. McVeagh had used nitromethane as one of the agents, but Sam thought that his formula was superior. He checked his watch, it was 10.37 a.m.

Because the police had agreed to keep Kings U3A up to date with any developments, Clapham rang Ron Barber to advise him of the murder overnight in Southside.

"So, the son of a bitch is still alive," said Barber, when he heard the news. "We have a meeting today to elect a new president. The members will be shattered to learn about this, just when we all thought the bloody nightmare was over."

"What time is the meeting, Mr Barber?"

"2 p.m. at the usual place. I'm expecting about 150 to attend. We always put on afternoon tea for this sort of thing, it guarantees a good turnout."

"Maybe I should put in an appearance, just to assure your members that we are still following every lead in the case, now that we know who we are looking for."

"Damn good idea, Detective," said Barber. "The realisation that the bastard is still somewhere around here is a chilling thought. Come over a few minutes before two, and I'll look out for you."

Clapham put down his phone.

What do you say to the terrified locals when yet another murder occurs, and you the policeman have nothing to offer, except that you now know who you are looking for?

Barry had been busy, writing yet another piece of copy about the latest killing, when he got Tommy's call.

"Barry, why didn't you call me about the latest murder? I just heard about it on the radio!"

"Sorry Tommy, I monitor the police radio, and shot over to Southside early on when I heard about it."

"Okay, well I am on my way there now to check out the address of a fellow who may have a connection to our killer. Why don't you join me? I'll meet you at the Southside Post Office, say eleven o'clock?"

"No problem," said Barry, "see you there."

Tommy found a park some distance from the Post Office, and as he approached, he saw the red Corolla. Barry had found a park right outside.

"You should buy a lottery ticket, mate," said Tommy, as he got into the Corolla.

"What now?" asked Barry.

Tommy explained about the result of his visit to the council office.

"You mean Cook may have a friend? That's bloody unusual."

"That's what I thought. Let's drive past number forty-six Langton Drive. Corollas are pretty common, so if we drive slowly, nobody will notice."

Barry took offence. "Do you mean common as in common , or just plain common?"

"You know what I mean Barry, now let's go."

Just as number forty-six came into view, a Honda Accord started reversing out of the driveway.

"Stop Barry!" exclaimed Tommy, "let him go. I'll get the plate number and check with the office to confirm that it belongs to this Mr Charlton."

Barry stopped the car about seventy yards from the house. Fortunately they were on the opposite side of the road. The Honda drove past them without a glance from the driver, who was wearing a beanie and sunglasses. A bicycle was attached to a brace on the rear of the car.

"Who goes cycling late morning on a weekday?" said Tommy. "Let's follow him, just out of curiosity."

Neither of them noticed that behind a large white delivery van travelling in the opposite direction was a red Alfa Romeo sedan with three occupants.

Tommy phoned his office to check the plate number of the Accord. He was pleased that the insurance industry had access to this official facility, as it removed any doubt about vehicle ownership when it came time for claims.

The traffic got a little heavier as the Honda threaded its way out of Southside.

"Looks like he may be going towards Kings, Barry. Keep well back, we don't want to be spotted."

Not far from the Kings hall they got a red light, and the Honda disappeared, turning off to the left.

"Go slowly Barry, I think that he may have turned towards the hall, it's only three blocks down there."

The Kings traffic lights were not synchronised, and they got another red.

Tommy's phone rang.

"Yes, this is Tomlinson. What? That can't be right? Say it again, this time more slowly please. You say that the number that I gave you is registered to a Mr Samuel Cook, for a black Lexus 350GS? Yes, thank you, I got it."

Tommy's mind was racing. Bicycles, Hondas, a black Lexus. Could it be?

"Barry, there has been a plate switch between Cook's Lexus and the Honda Accord. Only one person could have done that, and that's Cook. The Lexus must now have the plate belonging to the Honda."

Five minutes later, as they drove past the hall, the Honda drove out of the carpark next to the large public park behind the hall, going in the opposite direction. Tommy ducked down.

"Barry, something is wrong. He has dropped off the bike. How bloody peculiar."

"Shit, you're right. He didn't hang around, maybe he just wanted to dump it?" said Barry.

"Right, let's go straight back so we can check if he went home again."

It was 11.45 when Tommy and Barry drove past number forty-six Langton Drive.

The Honda was parked on the driveway, minus the bicycle.

"So a stranger with some loose connection to Cook drives all the way from his house in Southside to a park in Kings, just to dump a bike? Am I missing something Barry? I am going to ring Clapham. He should know what we have found out."

Thirty minutes later, Sam Cook moved the Honda off the driveway before driving out a white Lexus. He then put the Honda in the garage and closed the door. After checking the house one last time, he drove well away from Southside to fill the petrol tank of the Lexus. Seventy litres of premium grade gasoline would, when vaporised by the bomb, add to the spectacle. He thought that it would have been more spectacular at night, but the scene was set.

At 12.30 p.m., Detective Clapham arrived at the house in Langton Drive with a search warrant, and a contingent of heavily armed members of the Emergency Response Team.

Loud knocking on the front door of the house drew no response, so a battering ram was used to smash the lock. The squad rushed the house, going from room to room, shouting warnings, but the place was empty. In the garage, they found a Honda Accord. In a rear bedroom, they found a small but very sophisticated P lab, with enough chemicals to supply the drug market for months.

What alarmed Clapham the most was the pile of empty bags labelled 'ammonium nitrate' on the floor around the work bench. That, and the empty spray cans of white enamel scattered around. What had Cook been painting? Then it struck him, of course, the bastard had most likely repainted his car.

He immediately put out a red alert for either a black or white Lexus, probably being driven by Samuel Cook, the man wanted for the Kings killings. The public were to be advised that he may be armed, and was not to be approached. Somewhere during his training, Clapham had learned that ammonium nitrate could be used as a base chemical in the manufacture of a very potent bomb. He rang Rossiter. It took some minutes to get him on the line.

"Be quick Clapham, I am waiting a call from the Minister."

"Sir, Cook is on the loose, possibly in Kings or Southside, driving a black or possibly white Lexus, which I now believe to be carrying a bomb. We found evidence that he may have processed a large amount of ammonium nitrate in his garage, and at the same time repainted his car. I have put out a red alert."

"Fuck it Clapham, it's time to mobilise the entire force, and call in the bloody army. This murderous madman could be about to bomb the bloody station, the mayor's office or the bloody Kings Mall. I'll get the message repeated to all media. The bastards want a story, let's see what they can do with this."

It was 1 p.m.

With the Lexus fully fuelled, Cook decided to have lunch at a nearby café.

Chapter Forty-six

As he sat quietly mulling over his plan, Sam was more than pleased with the quality of his latest batch of P. He felt he had struck the right balance for his own use. Now that he had decided that the U3A meeting scheduled for that afternoon would be the ideal time to punish all of the Kings U3A membership at the one time, he had become very excited.

He had discussed his plan with Amelia the night before, and he thought she had agreed. He was pleased she had forgiven him for the fire at Collectibles, even though she had been forced to lose her privacy.

The stupid police were hunting for a black Lexus. They won't pay much attention to a white one, he thought. It had taken hours to mask up the car prior to painting, but it had been worth it. The finished job was not totally professional, but Sam thought it was good enough.

The car bomb, according to his calculations, would totally destroy everything within a hundred yard radius of the Kings church hall. He had set the timer for 2.14 p.m. All he had to do now was switch on the activator. His heart was racing as the P he had administered to himself was now intensifying the feeling in him of an almost godlike superiority, and at the same time suppressing any feelings of moral responsibility. He was hallucinating, already picturing the scenes of destruction and carnage that he was about to visit on those attending the meeting.

He would park the car behind the hall at 2.05, activate the bomb, lock the car, retrieve the bike from the park where he had chained it to a tree, and ride it to the local railway station. There, he had deposited in a rented locker all the necessary items for his overseas holiday. His new passport, issued in the name of a child who died at birth more than fifty years ago, had

cost him only five thousand pounds. The child's name was
Frank Van den Broeke. Cook thought Amelia would like the
South African connotation.

Chapter Forty-seven

Clapham sat in the main briefing room with Rossiter and other senior staff. Rossiter was standing by a map fixed onto a white board.

"So what we know is that Cook has most likely made a bomb, and with the amount of planning he has put into it, we can assume he intends to use it, and soon. We think his Lexus will be the container, because of the amount of ammonium nitrate which has been revealed by the number of empty bags found at his hideout. The question is, what, and where, is his bloody target?"

Clapham jumped to his feet.

"It must be the U3A meeting today at 2 p.m. I'm supposed to be addressing them for an update. They're expecting about 150 members to show up."

Rossiter first went pale, then into overdrive. He stared at the ten men and women in the room.

"Mobilise everyone you can and get down to the hall. Get the meeting abandoned, put out a cordon and clear the area. Call in all available units and close all the streets in the immediate vicinity of the hall. You are now authorised to fire on any Lexus that does not stop when requested. I will alert the bomb squad and advise the Minister. Cook must be stopped at all costs."

The room quickly emptied as a red alert went out to all mobile units to make haste to the Kings' Hall area, where Sam Cook, aka Henry Charlton, a suspected bomber, was on the loose, thought to be driving either a black or white Lexus 350 GS.

Shortly after one-thirty, Cook scooped the last of the chocolate foam from his coffee cup and left the café.

As he approached the car, he heard hurried steps behind him. He turned to face a trio of young people, now only three or four yards away. A woman and two men, all three wearing sunglasses.

Sam Cook did not like surprises. Every day of his life was planned and detailed, or had been until now.

"Ello, Mezzda Cook, remember me?"

For a moment Cook was in shock.

Then he recognised Violetta Cavalli.

"Violetta, what are you doing here?" he stammered. "I'm very busy right now. Maybe we could meet for a coffee later?"

"No, we want to talk to you now. It's about the death of my dear friend Adolpho, which occurred while you were in Stresa. The coroner found that he was dead before his Maserati went into the lake. You are coming with us."

As she spoke, one of the men stepped forward to grab Cook by the arm. It was a mistake. Cook swung around aiming his left hand for a blow to the man's throat. He missed his target but the blow landed sharply across the man's temple, and silently he crumpled to the ground.

Cook pushed Violetta towards the other man, who now had a switchblade knife in his hand. The man hesitated for a moment, giving Cook time to get to the door of the Lexus, which was opened by his electronic proximity key. He got in just as his attacker slashed at his right shoulder, finding only the shoulder pad of his jacket. Cook hit the security button locking the car, and started the engine.

He looked up to see Violetta standing in front of the car aiming a small pistol directly at him. He slammed his foot on the accelerator, and the Lexus leapt forward knocking her away before she could fire. With his heart racing at the exertion he slowed down momentarily, but then sped up as he realised that the Italians would give chase.

Checking the dashboard clock, he realised that his schedule was now under threat. His priority now was to lose his pursuers. He decided to drive well out of town, checking every few seconds to see if there was a car chasing him. After ten minutes he pulled into a side road, stopped and listened. Nothing.

Cook thought about the arrogant Italian playboy who had tried to trick him over a minor drug deal. He decided that Violetta had made a poor choice mixing with Adolpho Galleotti. He must have been her lover.

Turning on the radio, he caught the end of a news item warning the public to be on the lookout for a black or white Lexus. It was thought to be driven by Samuel Cook, the notorious Kings serial killer. It went on to warn the public not to approach him if he was seen, but to immediately call the special police Crimestoppers number.

Suddenly reality struck him. He checked the clock again. It was six minutes to two. His plan had gone awry. He'd have to disable the timer for the bomb while he reviewed the situation.

An idea came to him. He would disappear. He had done it once. Yes, let the bastards think he was dead. Then after a suitable time, when calm had been restored, he'd strike. He hadn't finished with Kings U3A yet. With the timer reset for three p.m. he drove off. There was no sign of the red Alfa.

Chapter Forty-eight

By three minutes to two o'clock, the Kings Hall area had been cleared and a wide police cordon had been put in place. The members of U3A expecting to attend a meeting had been dispersed and sent home.

Rossiter and Clapham stood in the carpark talking to the leader of an Armed Offenders Squad who had arrived by helicopter. They quickly brought him up to date with the events of the last hour, and informed him of the possibility of a car bomb being detonated somewhere in the general area.

But despite the warnings to all police in the country, and to the public by radio and social media, there were no sightings of the wanted Lexus or its occupant Mr Samuel Cook.

"Our friend must have gone to ground, Clapham. He would have heard the alerts by now, but I can't understand why his car hasn't been spotted yet," said Rossiter. "Maybe one of our police Eagle helicopter patrols will find him."

"Sir," said the AOS Senior Sergeant, "our orders are to stay on site with you until some resolution is found or circumstances change."

Rossiter nodded in acknowledgement.

Cook, having made his decision, was driving on secondary roads heading for a small railway station some distance in the opposite direction to Kings. Once there, he parked the Lexus alongside a rake of old wagons. They would provide a shield for anyone looking from the platform. Behind them was a stand of overgrown trees and hedges, a near-perfect hiding place.

Satisfied that it was quiet enough, Cook quickly checked the timer again, locked the Lexus, and quietly made his way to the station.

There were only four or five people waiting for the next local train and nobody noticed the man in the dark clothing, wearing sunglasses and beanie, and carrying a small backpack. He bought his ticket from the dispenser and sat down to wait.

The local train had only four carriages, and he found one at the rear which was almost empty.

Twenty-five minutes later, alighting at Kings Station, he went to the men's room and sat in an empty stall. He removed his beanie, and reaching into his backpack, he swapped it for a peaked cap. He checked his watch. It was 2.57.

Not long now, he thought to himself.

A man entered, relieved himself, and left.

It came first as a dull thud, then a distant roar. Then a moment's silence followed by shouting, and footsteps here and there. Cook stepped out onto the platform. People were standing staring at the huge column of smoke rising in the distance.

"Bloody hell!" exclaimed one man, "must have been a World War Two bomb gone off."

"Probably," agreed Cook, before walking into the left luggage room to retrieve his wheeled case, just in time to catch the next train.

Chapter Forty-nine

Three months later, the interim official report released by the Minister of Police concluded that Mr Samuel Cook, who had been the chief suspect in the spate of killings in the Kings area, was also responsible for the explosion at the Redwood Railway Station.

A detailed forensic examination of the site had found no human remains. An engine block and part of an axle found approximately two hundred yards from the crater created by the blast were identified as having come from a Lexus sedan. Five derelict railway wagons had also been destroyed, with only some of the wheels and bogies remaining. The crater created by the explosion was twelve feet deep, and almost fifty feet in diameter. The conclusion was that Cook, knowing he was wanted by the police, had decided to take his own life. His body had been vaporised in the huge blast.

The Minister thanked the Kings Police team for their work in identifying Cook as the serial killer who had been stalking the town and its residents. The investigation could now be wound down. The citizens of Kings and the surrounding area could now go about their business without the fear of attack. The dark cloud of foreboding which had shrouded their lives for the past year had been removed.

Chapter Fifty

Since the Berlin Wall came down, bringing the Soviet Union down with it, Amelia had always wanted to visit the Baltic Countries. They were so close, she had observed to Sam on many occasions, yet one heard very little about them.

Cook thought it was unfortunate that she was not able to be with him as he wandered through the Old Town precinct of Tallinnn, the capital of Estonia. He marvelled at the host of little shops displaying jewellery made from the natural gum of ancient trees garnered from the seashore. Amber had been prized through the centuries for its unique adaptability and variety for use as jewellery.

But today, Cook did not have jewellery on his mind. He was looking for a stamp dealer. Hopefully, with Tallinnn's position as a gateway to both the Nordic countries and Russia, he thought he would be able to find one who dealt in the international market.

It didn't take him long to find just what he was hoping for. There, tucked on the corner of a narrow lane, he spotted a window sign, 'Stamps International'. As he approached, he read the name of the proprietors in gold lettering, 'Josef Hlavacek & Son'.

As he opened the door to the shop a small bell tinkled above his head. He glanced around, thinking this was what he had always wanted Collectibles, his now defunct shop, to look like. It must have been at least two hundred years old, with faded oak panelling, parquet flooring, and brass-hinged cupboards. A young man was sitting on a high stool in front of a sloping table looking at a large bound book. Cook thought it would be a stamp collection.

Looking up, he smiled at Cook.

"*Guten Tag.*"

"Do you speak English?" asked Cook, noting the name Miroslav Hlavacek on the name tag the man was wearing

"Yes, I'm sorry sir, at first glance I thought you were German. We don't get so many visitors from the UK."

"Well, I am here for a short break. I have been rather busy lately, and your country has always been a kind of mystery to me."

"That's not unusual, Sir, we enjoy our low profile. We are a well-kept secret when it comes to holiday destinations. What can I do for you today?"

"I have a small collection of Russian stamps as well as stamps from the Baltic, and the former East Prussia, which I would like to sell. Would you be interested in looking at them?"

"We certainly would. We have a New York office, and interest in stamps from this part of the world has been growing since the political change. We have regular auctions which attract attention from all over the world. If you make an appointment, I can make sure that my father is on hand to help with a valuation. You can see from our name that we are from the Czech Republic, where we also maintain a small shop."

Agreeing to return the following afternoon at two, Mr Van den Broeke continued sightseeing.

Chapter Fifty-one

Tommy Tomlinson was sitting at the little desk he had brought with him when he had moved into Lynda Osborne's home as a boarder. Life in Kings had returned to the rather quiet, mundane pace which appealed to the largely greying inhabitants of the area. Everyone acknowledged that the horror which Samuel Cook had visited on the town would remain as a dark shadow for years to come, but they were determined not to let it ruin the spirit of unity which the episode had created.

The doors of the large grey cabinet where Tommy kept his precious stamp collection were open, as he quietly scrolled through the international stamp auction sites on his laptop. Open on the bed, next to the desk, was the printout of the catalogue of stamps which Alfred, the deceased husband of Jean Adams, had registered with an insurance company. None of the collection had ever been found, but Tommy remained convinced that if they had not been lost in the conflagration at Collectibles, then they would eventually surface somewhere, because of their value. Besides, he felt that he was still involved with them because the reward offered was still unclaimed.

He was looking at a collection of Russian stamps being offered by a small New York auction house when a particular brown stamp caught his eye. It was a 1934 5k commemorative of Lenin's death, featuring his mausoleum. It looked vaguely familiar. He took down one of his albums which contained a few eastern European and Russian stamps. He carefully turned the four specialised pages, but could not find what he was looking for. In a quandary, he picked up the insurance printout and ran his finger down the index looking for the eastern European section.

It was limited to less than a dozen descriptions, but one was for a Russian brown 1934 5k with Lenin's mausoleum.

Tommy was relieved to confirm that his memory was not playing tricks on him after all, but he was startled to read that because the stamp was from a rare imperfect sheet, it had a value of $22,000.

He checked the description of the next stamp on the list. It was described as "a Consular Poltinnik" A rare 50-kopek Russian consular tax stamp with an overprint "Air Post 1200 germ. Marks". He returned to the laptop to check the auction house offering. There it was. Estimated value $75,000.

According to the catalogue, its release was not coordinated with the People's Commissar at the time, and it was soon withdrawn. Only 50-75 were preserved.

Twenty minutes later, shaking with excitement, Tommy had identified all of the eastern European collection from the insurance information. They had a combined value of over $265,000. Someone was selling the Adam's collection. Could it be that Cook was still alive?

Returning to his laptop he clicked on the home button of the auctioneers. A small chart explained that the company was owned by the Hlavacek family from the Czech Republic, who had moved their head office to Tallinnn, Estonia some years ago, but still retained a business in Prague as well as the New York operation. The principal's name was Josef Hlavacek. Tommy quickly concluded it would probably be good business to offer the valuable collection he was looking at in New York rather than Tallinnn, given the number of philatelists in the USA.

He checked his watch. It was 3 p.m. His early naval training in navigation and time zones told him that it was five p.m.in Tallinn.

Miroslav Hlavacek answered the call. Tommy asked to speak to the manager, and when Hlavacek Jnr. quickly explained his role, the conversation continued. Tommy used his insurance persona as a reason for the call 'in connection with the disappearance of the Adam's collection.'

Hlavacek was quick to defend his business.

"Sir, we are proud of our reputation over many years in business. It is not possible for us not to have provenance on everything that we offer. Otherwise we would have no business. The world of philately is always protecting its ethics."

"I apologise," said Tommy, "I had no intention of impugning your company. I am just curious about how the collection came into your hands."

"Sir, all I can say is that the seller, whose name I cannot divulge, produced all the bona fides which we demand before entering into a contract. Beyond that, I'm afraid I cannot help you." At that, the phone went dead.

"Well I'll be damned," Tommy whispered to himself. "The Adams' stamps have not only survived, but they have been whisked well away from home. To Tallinn of all places. How very strange."

He turned back to his laptop to check the email address of Mark James, his old colleague in London, who had contacted him about the stamp theft months before, offering him a substantial reward for their return.

Mark James smiled when he read Tommy's email later that day.

It read, 'Stamps about to be towed out of danger. Taking a tug toTallinn. Get ready to receive details of my bank account for reward. Casting off, Tommy.'

It was the kind of cryptic message he would expect from an old salt like Tommy.

Barry Smart was really puzzled when Tommy gave him the news that he was off to Tallinn.

"Help me Tommy, where the hell is Tallinn?'

"Not far from Riga," Tommy replied, as they quietly sat at the Goh coffee shop. "It's on the Baltic, Barry. I must have taken a ship in there a dozen times."

He watched Barry's eyes widen as he explained his theory that Cook may have fled to the Baltic, and was trying to cash in on the stolen stamps.

"I'm off tomorrow morning. With any luck, I may have that exclusive story you have been looking for."

As they shook hands, Barry became very serious.

"You take care over there Tommy. I have heard some very nasty stories about the Russian Mafia being active."

"I'm overdue for a little excitement," said Tommy, as they parted.

Chapter Fifty-two

The airport at Tallinn had not quite recovered from the days of Soviet occupation, but the new Olympia hotel brought back many happy memories for Tommy, as he took the one step up from the lobby entrance and walked across the grey marble floor to reception. At the buffet the breakfast plates piled with smoked salmon were legendary, and the hotel was within comfortable walking distance from the old town. For confirmation, he had Googled the address of the stamp shop of Hlavacek & Son, and found it to be just as he remembered it, off the main square.

Hlavacek smiled as he recognised the old customer at the counter.

"Captain Toms, where have you been? How many years is it?"

"Too many," replied Tommy, "far too many, Josef, my old friend. I am spending some time ashore, as I had what the shipping company called 'a lapse of judgment'."

"I won't ask what that was, Captain. Not a woman I suppose?" Joseph asked with an evil grin.

"Josef, I'm working for an insurance company who are looking for a stamp collection, stolen back home at the same time that a murder was committed. I think some of the stamps may be in your latest auction catalogue offered by your New York office."

Josef raised his eyebrows. He knew Captain Toms was serious.

"What are you saying, Captain? You think I would deal in stolen property?"

"No, no, no Josef. Not you, but maybe one of your clients?"

"You remember my son Miroslav, Captain? He is, what do you say in English, a nerd? He looks after all the records on his computer."

Joseph pressed a button under the counter, and his son appeared.

"Miroslav, do you remember our old friend Captain Toms? He is looking for a thief."

"Well Pop, he has come to the right place. I remember how you used to steal stamps from old ladies back home in Prague," he said, winking at Tommy. "Nice to see you again, Captain."

"Miro, he is asking about some of the stamps in the New York catalogue for the end of the month auction."

"Oh those. They are on commission from that South African guy. Just a minute and I'll check his name," he said moving to a computer terminal on the counter.

"Here you go, his name is Van den Broeke, you can't be more South African than that. I also have his passport number."

"Joseph, can we go into your office?" said Tommy. "I want to show you the connection between the stamps in your sale, and those on the missing list. I just don't believe in coincidences when it comes to rare stamps."

One hour later, Tommy, deep in thought, left the premises of Josef Hlavacek and Son. He didn't notice the man in the beanie and long leather coat, standing on the opposite corner. As a precaution fed by paranoia, Sam Cook had been waiting for the Stamps International shop to become empty before he entered. Cook was startled, but his caution had paid off. In a flash, he recognised that prying bloody insurance man from Kings U3A whose name he couldn't recall. What on earth could he be doing in a stamp shop in Tallinn, thought Cook? Is he following me? What does he know?

He followed him at a discreet distance, out of the square, across the main road, dodging trams, through the park, and finally watched him enter the Olympia Hotel. The bastard may have got away during their last encounter, he thought, but the next time we meet, he is going to die.

Chapter Fifty-three

Cook was having difficulty getting supplies of P, and at the same time keeping an eye on his budget whilst waiting for the outcome of the New York auction. On his arrival in Tallinn he had quickly found out that the drug supply in the country was controlled by a Russian gang operating out of Riga, the main town in Latvia. It shared a border with both Estonia to the north and Lithuania to the south. All three had a coastal connection with the Baltic Sea to the west, and Russia to the east. It was a perfect hub for the import and distribution of a whole catalogue of legal and illegal drugs. Fake prescription medicines were sold at prices undercutting the legitimate suppliers, and stand-over tactics by the gang forced many smaller retail chemists to stock a percentage of the suspect products.

Cook had found a supplier at a bar in the Old Town, and was surprised that the transaction took place out in the open. His source had assured him, with a wink, that the police were 'sympathetic' to his activities.

Walking back to his own hotel, he could feel the sense of outrage welling up inside. He began to rhythmically chop his left hand into his right. The exercise always calmed him, but only a little. Driven by paranoia, and haunted by ever increasing delusions, he now saw a conspiracy being mounted against him by the U3A man, whose name he couldn't remember, and the Czech father and son. He had put aside a large amount of money over time, but he had been counting on the proceeds of the sale of the stolen stamps to help finance not only his travels, but also the cost of setting up a new manufacturing lab on his return home. His Swiss lawyer had advised him that the proceeds of the claim against the destruction of his block of shops in Kings had been paid into his Swiss trust account, but he viewed this account as his retirement fund.

By the time he reached his hotel he had settled on a plan. Any threat to him, real or imagined, posed by the presence of the U3A man, had to be quickly removed.

Meanwhile, back at the Olympia Hotel and armed with the knowledge that Sam Cook was in Tallinn masquerading under the name of Frank Van den Broeke, Tommy decided there was much more at stake than the recovery of the stolen stamps. He finished his gin and tonic at the bar and made his way back to his room.

He called Barry Smart with the news of his discovery, and asked him to take all the details, which he dictated to the young reporter, to Detective Guy Clapham.

Smart could not believe his luck. He had been handed access to the biggest news story of his fledgling career. His heart pounding with excitement, he parked the Corolla in the visitors' area of the Kings police station and flew up the steps to the front counter.

The old desk sergeant, who in the past had shown a low level of tolerance to all members of the media, surprised Barry with the hint of a smile when he asked for Clapham.

"I hear that you have made an honest woman of our Constable Banks, Barry. You'd better go carefully mate, because you have got the whole of the Kings force watching you now."

Barry swallowed, and was pleased that Clapham walked through the door at that moment.

"What's up Barry, cat up a tree?"

"No, Mr Clapham, something really serious. Can we go into an office?"

With the door of the interview room closed, Barry took out his notebook and repeated Tommy's message to the detective.

Clapham's eyes flashed with excitement.

"So Tomlinson's chasing the reward for the stamps stolen in the Adams' murder inquiry, and just happens across Mr Sam Cook alive and well in Tallinn? Good God, what a break!"

"Well he hasn't actually seen him, but the shop owner's description was enough for Tommy," said Barry, "and the alias he is using has a South African connection. Remember his poor wife was from there."

"Van den Broeke, you say?" asked Clapham, taking out a notebook.

"That's right. Obviously the miserable bastard has got himself a new passport."

"Well I'll have to report higher up, Barry. This is now something for Interpol. Cook is a homicidal maniac. If he spots Tomlinson, then your friend's life is in immediate danger, but I'm sure that he realises that."

"What next then, Detective?"

"Leave it to me Barry. I can see an international dragnet going into action within the hour, once Rossiter hears what I have to say. Thanks for coming in. You had better get back on the phone to Tomlinson and tell him to lie low until Cook is cornered."

Once back at his desk at the *Kings Herald* newspaper, Smart began hammering out a draft news release on his Apple Mac. He wanted to use the scoop to establish his journalistic abilities, not only with the editor, but also with the *Herald* readers.

He agonised over a choice of headline. "Kings Killer Traced To a Baltic Hideout" – "U3A Serial Killer Seen in Baltic Area" – "Sam Cook Cornered in Estonia".

Barry knew his editor was great at composing headlines, so with enthusiasm fuelled by a rush of adrenalin, he continued to weave his story using the information passed to him by Tomlinson. The headline could wait.

One hour later, the editor arrived at the Kings office intrigued by Barry's call to him. He had never heard his charge so excited.

"So, Barry, what's up? You said you have a real story?"

Barry quickly recounted the gist of Tomlinson's call and handed the man his draft article.

"What about the cops?" he asked, looking at Barry.

"Clapham said that he would tell Rossiter, who he thought would alert Interpol."

"Great stuff Barry, let's go. We have a special edition to get out."

Four hours later a special edition of the *Kings Herald* was distributed to the usual outlets. The banner headline read 'Cook Alive and Hiding in the Baltics'. The byline read that the scoop was the work of investigative journalist Barry Smart. The effect on those reading the story was immediate. Cell phones everywhere signalled an alert, and within minutes, a pall of horror settled on a community which had been gradually accepting the now false reality that Cook was dead. Now all that had changed in an instant, the killer was still on the loose, and only one question remained.

Would he terrorise Kings again?

Chapter Fifty-four

Using his U3A password, Cook was quickly able to access the names of the members of his group on the Kings U3A homepage. His memory settled on the name Tomlinson when it came up.

Got you, you bastard, he smiled to himself. He rang the Olympia Hotel to check if Tommy was still staying there.

"I am sorry sir, but Mr Tomlinson checked out this morning," said the operator in answer to his question.

Cook slammed down the phone and rang Hlavacek's shop, Stamps International. Miroslav Hlavacek answered.

Cook enquired about the state of the auction, which had been held the previous day in New York.

Hlavacek said that things had gone well, but there were one or two technical aspects about delivery which they wanted to discuss with Cook.

"What bloody technical aspects? What are you talking about?"

Hlavacek could sense the man's rage over the phone, but remained calm.

"Sorry for the inconvenience Mr Van den Broeke. What time would you like to drop by the shop? I'll make sure that my father is here to see you."

Cook hesitated. He was confused and breathing heavily as his frustration grew.

"I can come at noon, and you better have a good explanation, because I want my money right now. Do you understand?"

"Yes, Mr Van den Broeke, we will wait for you at noon. Thank you for calling."

Hlavacek immediately rang the Tallinn Police Headquarters and spoke to the detective who had been alerted by Interpol that a serial killer was loose in Tallinn. When they had visited Stamps International, the police had told the Hlavaceks that Van den Broeke was wanted for the theft of the stamps. They did not mention that he was a serial killer.

At eleven o'clock, an old man with a walking stick and carrying a small backpack took a seat in a café on the corner of the square in the Old Town across from Stamps International. He wore sunglasses and a French beret. He ordered coffee and a bread roll with herring. Except to the waiter who took his order, the man was more or less invisible.

Shortly after 11.25, the old man glanced up from his newspaper to observe the arrival of two cars outside Stamps International. Three uniformed policemen alighted from the first car, a police Volvo. They were joined by three men in plain clothes from the other unmarked car, a BMW.

The six men disappeared into the shop, and the cars drove off.

At 11.30, the old man paid his bill, gathered his belongings, and walked slowly across the square. At the main road he stopped a taxi and asked to be taken to the Tallinn railway station.

The taxi driver, checking his passenger in the rear view mirror, wondered why he kept chopping his left hand into the palm of his right.

At the station, the old man bought a ticket on the next train to Riga. Faced with a wait of forty-five minutes, he found a copy of the *Times* of London at a kiosk, and settled in the waiting room.

On page seven, he was startled to read a small paragraph near the bottom of the page. It was headlined, 'Kings Serial Killer spotted in Baltic'. It went on to explain that a reliable source had reported the whereabouts of the killer, and that Interpol had been alerted. The news had created a tumult of concern in the Kings area, where the residents had previously assumed that the wanted man, Samuel Cook, had perished in an explosion.

The sleek modern train of six carriages slid quietly into the station, and Cook found a seat towards the rear. He was surprised at how roomy the carriages were, benefiting from the Russian legacy of broad tracks, laid down during the Cold War for transporting heavy tanks.

The guard took his ticket without glancing at him or speaking. The EU knew no borders, but he had a fake New Zealand passport, which he had acquired in Tallinn, ready just in case. It was in the name of Edgar James Wilson, a retired printer from Wellington.

The pine forests of Estonia soon gave way to the more cultivated look of Latvia.

The old man felt surprisingly calm as he began planning an assault on his old home town, one that the residents would never forget. He felt they had brought it upon themselves by prying into his private life with their small town gossip and petty jealousies. He had always felt superior to the lot of them, especially their stupid plodding policemen. But first he had business in Riga.

Personal business.

Chapter Fifty-five

Tommy Tomlinson was pleased to be home again. He had been right about the source of the stamps, Interpol had become involved in the search for Cook, and in due course he would get the reward for the return of the stolen stamps. How Cook had managed to evade the trap set for him at the Hlavacek's shop remained a mystery. Tommy speculated that the maniac may have fled into Russia, as he seemed to have access to sufficient funds to be able to travel at will.

The startling news that Cook was still alive had reawakened all the past anxieties suffered by the residents of Kings. The special meeting called by the police had gone some way to calm things down, but there was no doubt that the threat of his return was palpable in the community, and would remain so until he was finally caught.

Tommy's landlady, Mrs Osbourne, was more than delighted with the small amber brooch which he had brought back from his trip. She had been keen to know the reason for his trip, especially now that the papers were claiming that Sam Cook was thought to be somewhere in the Baltic area.

Tommy had smiled faintly when asked, and said that he had been attending to a little business.

Mrs O didn't pursue the matter.

James Rossiter and the other senior police officers were still smarting from the fact that they had let Cook slip through their fingers on the day of his attempt to blow up the local hall at the time of a U3A meeting. A disaster may have been averted, but the killer was still on the loose.

In response to the reported sighting, Rossiter instructed Guy Clapham, the local Kings detective, to reactivate the specialist squad which had been formed during the earlier investigations. They had been stood down several weeks after Cook disappeared.

The U3A committee for its part asked members to make sure they had updated all their contact numbers, and a group of volunteers was formed to call every member living alone, on a regular basis. A hotline contact to Clapham's squad was also circulated.

The official police position was that Cook had fled the country, and therefore the good people of Kings should have no fear of his return, and go about their business as usual.

At the next meeting of the U3A Wine Society, Ron Barber, who generally took a light-hearted view of life, was now more irascible.

"I'd say we are all in trouble till the bastard is caught. If you ask me, he will be like a bloody homing pigeon. He may have flown away, but mark my words, he'll be back. He may be as mad as a hatter, but he has shown himself to be resourceful and clever. He's got it in for us, for some reason. We should all be looking over our shoulders."

"Christ Ron, get a grip," said the convenor. "If the general membership hear you talking like that the whole place will be gripped by panic."

"It is already, said Barber, "they're just hiding it."

Chapter Fifty-six

Sam Cook found the clerk at the Riga branch of the Bank of Ukraine very helpful in assisting him to transfer funds from his Swiss bank account and turn them into euros. He said that such small amounts as Cook's seventy-five thousand euros were transacted every day by his many Russian clients from across the border, who used Riga for 'private purposes'. Sam was taken aback at the bank charge of three per cent of the total, but decided not to question it.

His contact in Tallinn had also given him an address where, the man had assured him, he could be put in touch with a cell of the Russian drug dealers who also had access to all kinds of military supplies which could be stolen to order from Russian military bases just across the border from Latvia.

What Cook had in mind for his return to Kings was to make a much smaller bomb than his previous attempt, and for that he needed a much more efficient explosive. As a chemist, he knew the reputation of the former Czech Republic for inventing Semtex, the forerunner of a new family of plastic explosives favoured by terrorists the world over. He had calculated that as little as two kilos would be sufficient for his purpose.

Two hours and two thousand euros later, Cook had placed his order. The dealer, who had described himself as being in the import/export trade, promised Cook delivery within twenty-four hours. Another two thousand euros would complete the transaction.

His next visit was to the Riga waterfront, where for one thousand euros he was able to get passage on trawler heading out into the North Sea, the next day. The captain assured him that he would be landed safely somewhere near Cromarty on the Scottish coast, a town Cook had never heard of.

The following afternoon, having collected his purchase from the Russian, he made his way to the waterfront.

Four days later, two of which Cook spent in a bunk suffering from sea-sickness, the captain told him to be ready to go ashore within thirty minutes.

Once on deck, Cook stared through the early morning mist at the cold grey coastline of Scotland with a feeling of relief. The sea quietened down in the shelter of the Cromarty Firth as a cutter about seven yards long drew alongside the trawler. It was made fast and the trawler crew started manhandling canvas-wrapped bales across to it.

"Away you go," the captain of the trawler yelled at Cook. He needed no urging to scramble awkwardly across into the cutter. He knew better than to ask what was in the bales, thankful that he would soon be on dry land.

The whole operation took less than five minutes, and five minutes later the trawler had disappeared into the mist. The three men on the cutter ignored him.

It glided quietly into a small inlet, where a large van stood waiting with the engine running. One of the crew helped Cook onto a rickety landing and pointed in the direction of a small signpost.

"There you go matey," he said, with a strong Scottish burr, "thirty minutes' walk, and you'll be in Cromarty. The pub opens at nine o'clock. Forget what you have seen, and you'll stay healthy. Understand?" He returned to the task of loading the van.

Cook understood, and trudged off towards the village.

The woman serving in the only café open was too hospitable for Cook's liking. He avoided most of her questions, but was grateful that she knew in reply to his enquiry that the bus to Inverness left at 10 o'clock, and connected with the main railway to the south.

The breakfast of bacon, eggs and chips was the best meal he had enjoyed since leaving Riga.

There were only three people on the bus. Forty-five minutes later, after three stops, with four more passengers joining the bus, it rolled into Inverness.

Cook bought a first class ticket for the nine-hour journey to London and relaxed at the station. He happily paid to use the washroom, and took the opportunity to clean himself up as best he could for the trip. The shower on the trawler had barely functioned, and he thought that the flask of cologne that he found at the station gift shop was a necessary investment.

As the tourist season had not yet arrived the express to London was only two-thirds occupied, so Cook was able to move about from time to time, keeping to himself as much as possible.

Arriving at Kings Cross, he quickly scanned the notice boards, and found a bed and breakfast offering on the outskirts of Wimbledon. The woman who answered his phone call said that she had a vacancy for the one night stay that he was planning on, so thirty minutes later, Mr Edgar Wilson, a visitor from New Zealand, was at her door.

He found the room was very good value as it had an en suite bathroom, allowing him his first hot bath in a week. After dinner at a nearby café, he retired for the night, and continued planning his visit to Kings.

The next morning he found a menswear shop and bought a modest wardrobe of bland new clothes including a wide-brimmed hat. He also bought a modern trolley suitcase which was more in keeping with his new persona. The purchase was completed with a new pair of sunglasses. Then he had a haircut, insisting that the barber cut his hair quite short. That afternoon, at a nearby pub, he ordered a half pint of ale, paying with a twenty-pound note and telling the barman to 'keep the change'. When asked, the man was only too happy to direct his benefactor to a young West Indian man sitting in a corner of the bar. After a visit to the man's car, Cook had bought enough P to last him for two weeks.

Less than five miles away, a young police trainee was absent-mindedly scrolling through the facial recognition tapes from various London stations taken in the previous five days. As an additional security measure after the terrorist attacks, they were part of the latest hi-tech surveillance system which had been installed across the city by the Metropolitan Police. He had been busy with the task for almost a week, and had spotted only one or two minor criminals including a small time drug dealer.

The tape he was running had been taken two days prior at Kings Cross Station. The machine suddenly sounded a number of beeps, and flashed up the face of a man on the 'most wanted' list. The trainee stared at the unkempt figure of an older man carrying a backpack.

The machine was flashing an ID number under the picture together with short description.

#79834867 : 8:46p.m.Samuel Cook aka Frank Van den Broeke. Wanted in connection with a series of murders at Kings.

He quickly read his sheet of procedures and rang his supervisor. The sighting was flashed to Scotland Yard, and also to the local Interpol office, although the matter was a case for the Yard.

A signal was then transmitted to every duty officer in the Greater London area. Samuel Cook, the serial killer from Kings, was at large in the great city.

The ticket office at Waterloo Station was, as usual, very busy when the well-dressed man towing a new trolley case approached the short queue. Cook hesitated for a moment when he saw a policeman standing adjacent to the window, but kept his place.

At the window the policeman stepped forward.

"Afternoon sir, where are you travelling to today?"

"I'm from New Zealand officer, and I'm going to visit friends."

The policeman smiled. "Go the All Blacks, eh?"

"What?" replied Cook, looking puzzled.

"Your rugby team sir, very famous over here you know."

"Oh yes, quite right, thank you," he murmured, as the policeman ran his eyes further down the queue.

With his ticket to the village of Littlewood Bridge situated twenty miles away from Kings, he noted the platform number, and breathing heavily, made for a nearby waiting room. He felt that he was in control once more.

On the train he found a seat in a carriage well towards the rear, where there were few passengers. An hour after the journey started, there only two youths left seated in the middle of the carriage, an old lady with a Zimmer frame at the front, with Cook in a seat beside the rear door.

One of the youths stood up, and staring at Cook, began to walk towards him. He suddenly produced a flick-blade knife and stood over Cook.

"Give me your fuckin' wallet or I'll cut you."

Cook hesitated. He saw that the other youth was now standing behind the first one, keeping watch.

"I have to stand up," said Cook.

"Fuck you," said the youth with the knife, as Cook got to his feet.

"Now give it to me, and stop screwing around," snarled the youth, pointing his knife at Cook's chest.

"All right, all right," said Cook, "just give me a moment."

Cook opened his jacket with his right hand, and began to reach into the jacket pocket with his left hand.

"Here you are," he said.

In a flash, the same hand slashed backhanded towards the youth's throat, and he dropped silent and wide-eyed to the floor, the knife sliding away under a seat. His companion turned and fled back down the carriage and through the door into the next one. Cook dragged the inert body on the floor to a position behind the nearest seat, gathered his belongings, and walked into the last carriage.

Three minutes later, the train made a scheduled stop and Cook alighted, walking unhurriedly to the nearest exit. No one had boarded, and the half-dozen others passengers who had left the train quickly dispersed as the train pulled out of the station.

Fifteen minutes later the Railway Police Office got an urgent call advising that a body had been discovered on the 3.46 from Waterloo station. A paramedic called to the scene had reported that the man appeared to have died from a broken neck.

Chapter Fifty-seven

Policewoman Louis Banks had been transferred back to the Kings Police station at Guy Clapham's request, because of her intimate knowledge of the area. She joined the group of six specialists in the reactivated search for Sam Cook, last seen at Waterloo Station.

When the news that a man had been found dead with a suspected broken neck on a train heading towards Kings, Assistant Commissioner Rossiter passed the message up the chain of command, where it eventually landed on the desk of the Minister of Police.

Once again, the order was given for substantial additions to the Kings police muster to be put into immediate effect. The U3A telephone trees were checked and updated so that all members were made aware of the avenues for assistance available to them.

The mood across the whole county was now bordering on hysteria, fuelled by widespread speculation that more killings were to be expected.

"They start off being angry, and then they become suicidal," said Clapham, referring to the mood of the public as he addressed his staff. "Assistant Commissioner Rossiter is the nominated person to speak to the press, and we expect to give them updates every morning at 9 a.m. until Cook is apprehended. If you thought the media were thick on the ground several weeks ago, it will be nothing compared to what is happening now. Inquiries are coming in from all across the EU as well as the United States. Do not speak to the press under any circumstances. We must portray an impression of calmness and professionalism at all times. We are going to get the bastard, and then you will be able to tell your grandkids that you took part in catching one of the most dangerous killers of modern times. You will all be rostered 24/7, stay alert and check every detail, no matter how trivial."

The car salesman at the Littlewood Bridge garage was only too happy to show the man the ubiquitous white Toyota van, which had a 'for sale' notice on it. He had taken it as a part-exchange on a new van from a local farming family. He started with the formula 'meet and greet' approach that he had been taught at the recent dealer meeting, and offered his hand.

He got a blank stare from the man.

"Just tell me the price, I haven't got all day," he said in a sharp tone.

Undeterred, the salesman began to recite the features of the vehicle.

The man began hitting his right palm with the edge of his left hand.

"Are you deaf? What is the price?"

The salesman stopped mid-sentence, seeing that his prospect was becoming agitated.

"Thank you sir, we are asking 1,995 pounds for the vehicle."

"I want a test drive."

"Certainly sir, I'll get the keys, if you will just wait a moment."

The salesman dashed into the small office.

"Rachel," he yelled at the ever-patient receptionist, "where did you put the bloody keys for the crappy old van we traded from the Frasers?"

"Right here, dopey." She smiled, holding up a small leather key wallet.

Once outside, the salesman handed the keys to the man, who had been walking around the vehicle.

The test drive took only about ten minutes, during which the salesman's efforts at small talk were met with silence. He began to feel very uncomfortable in the man's presence, and was pleased when they drove back into the yard.

Turning off the ignition, the man looked at the salesman, who for the first time noticed the man's cold almost detached stare.

"1,500 pounds. It's tired, but it will suit my purpose. Take it or leave it."

"Thank you sir, we have a deal," replied the salesman without hesitation. At that figure he would make a profit of 500 pounds. "If you will step into the office sir, we can do the paperwork."

Less than ten minutes later, the man who had identified himself as David Wilson had paid for the van in cash, and driven off. The salesman thought it a little strange that he had given a post office box number for an address, but a sale was a sale, and cash was king.

Sam Cook had decided a long time ago that he didn't like people. They showed him no respect.

He saw himself as educated, well-read, well-travelled, and able to argue on many topics, but still people remained distant. He had often discussed this matter with his wife, and her response was always the same. She said that people were jealous of him, they bore grudges, and lived petty, boring little lives.

In his mind, the members of Kings U3A epitomised everything that he detested. His effort to make a statement about his feelings for them at the last monthly meeting had been thwarted by bad luck. It was time to try again. This time the town would give him the respect that he deserved.

He drove the van to the tiny dilapidated cottage he had rented on the outskirts of Littlewood Bridge. He had paid the rent in cash, three months in advance, much to the delight of the older man who occupied a much larger house on the same piece of land, but some distance away. Cook needed privacy.

The cottage consisted of a bedroom, kitchen, a small lounge, plus a bathroom.

Carefully unwrapping his purchase from Riga on the kitchen table, he smiled as he saw the brick red colour of the Semtex showing through the plastic wrapping. There were several lines of Cyrillic writing on the label showing the contents to be of Russian origin. The four electronic detonators were contained in a small box. The simplicity of his planned weapon excited him. All he had to do was to somehow secrete it in the Kings Hall for the next U3A meeting. He would detonate the bomb electronically at a safe distance by using two cell phones.

Once he had achieved his objective he would go to South Africa, just as Amelia had suggested to him the last time he had consulted her.

While he was in Riga, he had checked the Kings U3A homepage to find out the date of the next meeting. It was scheduled for Monday the 23rd of November. Today was the 19th. He had four days to prepare. Placing the Semtex and detonators in his backpack he sat down to prepare a shopping list. First on the list was a bicycle. It would easily fit into the van, and added to the cloak of invisibility that he would need to plant the bomb. His experience had been that nobody seemed to notice older men riding bicycles. A dustcoat, overalls, and a hi-viz vest, he would find in the local charity shop. A torch and an extra cell phone, from a multi-purpose electronics booth he had seen at the railway station.

In the tiny bathroom, he checked on the disguise he intended to use. With dyed hair, self-correcting sunglasses, and a seaman's black peaked cap from the Baltic, Sam Cook, the shopkeeper from Collectibles, was unrecognisable.

He parked the van in the parking lot at the railway station and walked into the village.

The young man at the local bicycle shop was disappointed when Cook chose an old-fashioned bike, rejecting his suggestion that 'everyone was riding multi-purpose machines, these days'.

An hour later, he had found all the items on his shopping list, and with the old bicycle stored carefully in the back of the van, he drove back to the cottage.

It was Friday morning, and time to reconnoitre the Kings hall where the U3A monthly meeting was scheduled. Satisfied with his disguise, Cook set off in the van. He had decided to position it at the far side of the park, which reached to the hall about five hundred yards away. Unloading the bike, he put on the hi-viz vest over the overalls, and pedalled quietly across the park keeping to the cycle path. As he approached the hall he noticed two policemen standing to the side of the entrance. They returned his wave as he manoeuvred the bike off the cycle path and onto the road which led back around the park. A police van was parked on the other side of the hall. He wondered if the security presence was round the clock or just in daylight hours. Tonight he would check again.

At 1.37 a.m., the policeman on watch at the Kings hall was just pouring a cup of coffee from his Thermos when he noticed a man wearing a hi-viz vest riding past his police car. There was no moon, and the spotlight from the hall was rather weak. The policeman didn't bother to note the sighting, assuming that it was a shift worker returning home from the meat processing plant on the edge of the town. The coffee would keep him awake until he was relieved at 6 a.m.

Cook stopped some hundred yards into the park, slipped off the vest, and left the bike resting against a tree. He stood for a moment listening for any movement, then keeping to the tree line, he walked slowly towards the rear of the hall. Stopping twenty yards short of the building now looming out of the darkness, he checked again for any sound or movement.

Silence.

Starting off again, he prepared himself for the possibility of a motion activated light to come on. Nothing happened as he reached the rear of the building, so shielding the narrow beam of his penlight torch with his hand he found the exit doors. There were no exterior locks because they had to be activated from inside in case of emergency. Just to the side, he noticed a small louvered window which he guessed was a toilet. It was about six feet off the ground.

A plan was beginning to emerge. It would require some daring, but he didn't care, he was too committed to getting even with his enemies, either real or imagined.

Carefully treading his way back, he found the bike and pedalled quietly back to the parked van.

Chapter Fifty-eight

Louise Banks had been rostered onto the Kings police phones for Saturday morning from 8 a.m. to noon. Since the nationwide alert, three operators had been kept busy handling calls from the public offering information about the possible whereabouts of Sam Cook the serial killer. Every call was logged and recorded, and the detail then passed on to a large squad of detectives for follow-up and processing. It was laborious work, but everyone knew that the one vital call which could lead to the apprehension of the killer could come at any moment.

At 10.03 a.m. Louise took a call from a young woman who claimed to have seen a man acting strangely behind the Kings hall very early that morning. She and her boyfriend had been sitting on a park bench just inside the park when he passed behind them, coming from the hall. They thought it unusual that he was not walking on the path, which was lit. She preferred to remain anonymous, but felt that she should report what she had seen, because her boyfriend had said that it could be some pervert spying on courting couples in the park.

Louise thanked her, and logged the call and the recording. It would be assessed by one of the team.

Finishing her shift, she went to meet Barry, who had also arranged to have lunch with Tommy Tomlinson.

When she arrived at the café, Barry and Tommy were engaged in a deep conversation.

"I hope I am not interrupting you two," she said with a smile.

Both men made an effort to stand up, but she waved them away and bent down to kiss Barry on the cheek.

"What's the story?" said Barry.

"What story?" Louise tried to look puzzled.

"Take no notice Louise, he's trying to interrogate you again," said Tommy. "You know what reporters are like."

"Well if you must know," she replied, drawing her chair closer to the table and whispering, "I took a rather interesting call this morning."

Both men drew even closer to the table as she explained the information she had received.

Tommy took a deep breath. "My dear friends, we have a U3A meeting on Monday, and maybe there is a chance Cook will have another try. I am sure the police will be doing all that they can to keep the hall secure, but remember, we are dealing with a maniac, and a very intelligent and devious maniac."

Barry took Louise's hand. "Your caller gave no description at all?"

"No, she just said that she and her boyfriend thought it was an older man."

Tommy grimaced as he spoke. "If it is Cook, then we know he will be as high as a kite, if he has an attack in mind. The stuff he's taking will keep him awake for days, and feed his already dangerous paranoia. I hope the police are keeping an eye on his old haunts. I wouldn't be surprised if he has a stash of stuff somewhere in Kings."

"Clapham won't tolerate any amateurs getting involved Tommy, if that's what you're thinking. He would go nuts, and I'm sure that charges would result if he felt anyone was muddying the water. His whole career is in the balance since the first debacle. He has a lot to prove."

"I agree, but there is no harm in thinking about the situation, is there, Louise?" He glanced across at her for support.

"Tommy, are you still carrying that pistol you mentioned to me, some weeks ago?" asked Barry.

"I didn't hear that!" interrupted Louise. "I'm leaving. I'll call you later, darling," she said, as she stood up, blew Barry a kiss, and left the café.

"Now look what you've done, Barry. For God's sake, why mention my pistol in front of Louise?"

"Sorry, mate, silly thing to do."

"Ok then, let's leave it at that. I promise to leave the bastard to the police, but I'm still worried about Monday."

"I'll check with Clapham to see if he has anything to report," said Barry. "I'll call you if there is anything on the move."

They shook hands, and left the café in different directions.

Tommy's curiosity got the better of him, and he decided to drive past the house at 46 Langton Drive Southside, where he and Barry had seen Cook before his first failed attempt on the U3A meeting.

Sure enough, there was a police car parked outside the house. Opposite the police car was a rough old white van. Tommy dismissed it as belonging to a local tradesman, and continued on his way, pleased that the police had the house under surveillance. He was not to know that a policeman lay dead in the garage, and that Sam Cook was busy recovering a large plastic-covered slab of P that he had hidden in the garage wall weeks before. He was both surprised and delighted that the stupid police had not discovered it during their search of the property.

When the relief policeman arrived at the Langton Drive property at 3 p.m. he was horrified to find the body of his colleague on the floor of the garage, his larynx crushed and his neck broken. The man's hoarse emergency call to Kings police headquarters shattered the quiet routine buzz of the operations room, and set off a wave of shouted instructions, which to anyone standing by might have been interpreted as panic.

Sam Cook the serial killer had come home.

Chapter Fifty-nine

Barry Smart's interview with Detective Clapham was abruptly terminated, leaving Barry facing a dilemma. Should he stay at the station as an observer, or race back to the *Kings Herald*? He did neither. Instead he rang Tommy.

Tommy pulled his car over to take the call.

"Tommy, it's me, Barry. Cook has killed a policeman at the last house where you and I saw him. You know the one. There is uproar at the station..."

"Hold on Barry, I drove past the house half an hour ago. There was a tradesman's van parked opposite. What if...? Oh shit, I must have just missed him, if the van is his."

When the old white van stopped at the entrance to the Kings Hall at 2.41 p.m., the young policeman on duty asked the driver what he wanted. The man who was wearing tinted glasses, a cap, overalls, and a hi-viz vest, said the hall caretaker had called his company for a small repair to the water supply to the ladies' toilet. It seemed that some new washers were required, a job which normally would take only a few minutes.

The policeman directed the man to park at the side of the hall, and using his radio, alerted his colleague at the door of the hall that a plumber was coming in to fix a toilet.

The man entered the hall, nodded a greeting to the policeman, and made his way to the rear.

Seven minutes later, the man emerged from the hall making his way to the van.

"Job done then?" asked the young policeman.

"No problem," said the man, and slowly drove off. It was 2.51 p.m.

Cook was satisfied with his preparations. Using duct tape he had placed one bomb in the wash stand under the hand basin in the ladies toilet, and another behind a trap door under the main stage. He had calculated that two simultaneous blasts, fuelled in each case by one kilogram of Semtex, would blow the Kings Hall, and anyone within fifty yards of it, all the way to hell. He would be rid of all his enemies in one fell swoop. He felt inspired, euphoric even, almost the same as he had felt the day he had successfully manufactured Pervitin from the original formula.

Yes, Sam Cook was in charge again.

Five miles from Littlewood Bridge, Cook eased the old van into a disused barn he had found on the previous day. He lifted out the bicycle, removed the number plates from the van and placed them in his backpack. It took him less than ten minutes to cycle back to the cottage, where he would review his escape plan.

Barry Smart had immediately passed on to Clapham Tommy's sighting of the van at Southside. This had resulted in an immediate alert being flashed across the police frequency.

'Red alert, red alert, all staff, the wanted killer Samuel Cook has been sighted in the general area. May be driving an old white van, probably a Toyota Lite Ace. Check your cell phones for the latest description of the man. He is skilled in unarmed combat, and may be armed. If sighted, do not – repeat – do not approach him without backup. End of message.'

The young policeman on duty at the door to the Kings Hall heard the message and called out to his colleague standing by the carpark entrance.

"Hey Doug, that plumber was driving an old white van, shall I call it in?"

"Don't be bloody silly. Do serial killers wander around in hi-viz jackets? He was a bloody plumber for Christ's sake. You'll only make a fool of yourself. Anyway the dog squad have been all over the place today, and they didn't find anything."

"Ok, ok, I'm just saying, that's all," replied the young man. It was a decision that would later delay any thoughts that he had about an early promotion.

Assistant Commissioner Rossiter and Detective Clapham were sitting in the operations room with the team leader of the Armed Response team, and the Major in charge of the SAS squad who had been added to the search complement.

Rossiter was in charge of the total operation, reporting progress to the Commissioner every two hours. The Minister of Police thankfully had been deterred from coming to Kings for what Rossiter had termed 'a photo op'.

Standing at a whiteboard, he once again went over the arrangements that had been put in place to totally encircle Kings with roadblocks, CCTV, and unmarked cars. Ten plainclothes officers were on patrol along with thirty staff in uniform.

"The best outcome will be if the miserable bastard is confronted, raises a threatening hand, and is shot in self-defence by one of our men," he said.

"I hope it's me," said the SAS Major. "I'd give him the full magazine."

"You all know the rules of engagement," said Rossiter. "I don't have to tell you that the media are here in strength, and will be looking for any angle to sensationalise what is already being characterised as an example of incompetence by all involved, especially the Minister. You can bet your house that there will be a Commission of Inquiry. Anyway, let's get Cook this time, dead or alive, I don't care."

A few minutes later, the police call centre received a call from a woman who worked as a receptionist at car dealership in Littlewood Bridge. She said that her company had recently sold an old white farm van to a Mr. David Wilson for cash. She had no address for him, other than a post office box number in Redwood.

When he heard, Clapham slammed his fist on the table. "Typical bloody car dealer, slack records, just get the vehicle off the yard." Red with anger, he glared at the constable seated across from him. "You," he said, pointing his finger at the man, "remind me to get the trading licence taken off that bloody dealer when this is all over."

Chapter Sixty

With the whole area of Kings in a state of lock down, Tommy felt compelled to stay at home on Saturday night because Mrs O his landlady was in too high a nervous state to be left on her own.

She was more than happy to provide dinner for him, as she valued the calm demeanour he showed when everyone else seemed to be in a state of panic.

"They will get him this time, don't you think, Tommy?" she said as she brought in their dessert of strawberries and ice-cream.

"Yes, Mrs O, I am sure his time has come. The authorities are sparing no effort because it's unthinkable that he could come back to the area and not be apprehended. It would be the end of the Minister of Police, and possibly even the Government, if Cook somehow pulled another deadly attack."

After the meal, Mrs O settled down to watch her favourite TV show, and Tommy took his coffee to his room, explaining that he had 'a little business to attend to'.

Closing his door, he took a small case from his desk. It contained a set of navigational instruments that he had carried since his first day as a naval trainee.

He used dividers and a local road map to estimate the scale of a ten-mile radius using the Kings Hall as a centre point.

Because it had been assumed that Cook had escaped by train following his previous failed attempt, Tommy noted that Littlewood Bridge railway station was just on the ten-mile mark. The area between there and the hall was almost flat. A cyclist, for example, could comfortably cover the route in less than forty-five minutes. With the police presence at Kings railway station, Tommy wondered if Cook may have alighted from the train at Littlewood Bridge? If that was the case, then where was he hiding, if his plan was to attack the U3A meeting? Where could he lie low, unnoticed, until the time came for him to move?

He noted the Redwood Station, where Cook had detonated his first device, but it fell outside his present radius, and was on a secondary line.

Backpackers and B&B's could be discounted, because, he determined, the police would be watching all casual accommodation possibilities in the area. Maybe the maniac had reserved a house in advance, just as he had done over at Langton Drive, where he had hidden the Lexus?

Tommy sighed and went to look for more coffee.

Returning to his task a few minutes later, he once again pored over the road map. There were four roads leading into Kings. Two were rather circuitous, while the other two were more direct. To the north, one road had a more or less straight line towards Littlewood Bridge. The other, to the east, led to a forested area and ultimately to a National Park.

Discounting the possibility that Cook was already hiding somewhere in Kings, Tommy carefully perused the Kings-Littlewood Bridge road. As there were no points of interest noted, he guessed that the area along the road was all farming country. Had he turned the map over, he would have noticed that there were two or three tracks recommended for walkers and cyclists which criss-crossed the area, but they were not shown on the road map.

With the whole county now on the lookout for a white van, he assumed that Cook had by now dumped it somewhere. If he was not going to use the van as a car bomb, then he was either going to try to use some other means, or he had already placed a bomb in or near the hall, ready to detonate during the U3A meeting. Where would you dump a van out of sight, he wondered?

Then, almost without thinking, he took out the holstered pistol from the locked drawer in his desk.

He checked the safety catch and removed the magazine. It was a Glock 26, which held ten rounds, and had been recommended as a concealed weapon to many senior ships officers. Tommy had never fired it in anger, but had set up target practice from time to time in any ship which had a hold suitable for the purpose. It was in perfect condition, so replacing the magazine, he slid it back into the holster. He decided that he would continue to carry it until Cook was caught, despite Louise's disapproval.

Chapter Sixty-one

Dawn on that Monday morning came with a heavy fog which reduced visibility to only a few yards. Traffic was sparse, and any driver foolhardy enough or perhaps driven by necessity, inched along the road from Littlewood Bridge towards Kings with all lights showing. Even those with special fog lights were not much better off. Nobody noticed the lone cyclist making his way slowly along the cycle path which ran more or less parallel to the road but with a meandering separation of up to two hundred yards at times.

Constable Eion O'Connor had joined the force two years ago, because the O'Connors had always had a policeman in the family. He was standing under the lichgate at the entrance to St Patrick's Church, stamping his feet to keep warm as he waited for his relief, due in twenty minutes at seven a.m. There was a slight splash of water as the cyclist loomed out of the fog not more than thirty feet from him. Quickly flashing his torch, he yelled at the man.

"Hey, stop!"

· With that, the man responded by coming to a stop, balancing the bicycle with one foot on the ground.

"Where are you going?" asked O'Connor. "Do you have any ID?"

His face obscured by a big scarf and a cap, the man replied, "Yes I do, here hold my bike, and I'll get it out." He stepped off the bicycle.

O'Connor moved forward and took hold of the machine.

At seven a.m. O'Connor's replacement arrived at the church. The fog was still dense, helping to create an eerie feeling of apprehension across the churchyard.

"Are you there, O'Connor? It's Sergeant Andrews," he called, as he shone his torch around the area of the lichgate.

Getting no reply, he walked towards the church, just as the local priest came from the side, also flashing a torch.

"Good morning officer," he said cheerily. "Good to see all the security in place to catch this poor sinner."

"One of my team is supposed to be on duty here, have you seen anyone?

"No, Sergeant, but then I have just walked from the manse. If I had known that someone was on duty, I would have brought him a cup of tea."

"Could he be in the church?" asked the policeman.

"Quite possibly, we have a policy of never locking the door. God works 24/7 you know."

As they entered, the priest turned on the main lights in the church. He gasped. "There is someone asleep in the last pew."

The sergeant approached the dark-clothed figure leaning against the side of the pew.

"O'Connor, is that you? Wake up you lazy bugger," he said, pushing on the figure's shoulder.

The man slumped to the floor. The policeman shone his torch on the face of Constable Eion O'Connor.

"Holy Mother Mary," cried the priest, "he's dead."

"Bloody hell," said the policeman, pressing on his radio button.

Two minutes later an armed squad led by Detective Clapham was on its way to St Patricks.

It took only seconds of examination of the body for Clapham to conclude that with the bruising to O'Connor's throat and the angle of the head, Cook had struck again.

"The bastard's broken the cordon," he exclaimed. "I want a quick search of the area right now in case he's hiding in the vicinity."

"Guy, what about O'Connor's clothing? He would have been in uniform, not these civvies," observed the Sergeant, pointing at the old hat and coat on the body.

"Shit, it's only two and a half hours to the U3A meeting, and we have a serial killer probably masquerading as a policeman?"

He contacted Rossiter at HQ with the devastating news that not only had Cook penetrated the cordon around Kings, but he had at the same time murdered a young police officer.

As he walked to the door of the church, a squad member called to him.

"Hey, Guy, you'd better come and have a look at this."

Just outside the lichgate, the man was pointing to fresh cycle tracks, now visible as some sunlight had begun to penetrate the fog. Clapham could see that a bicycle had gone through a large puddle of water just short of the gate and splashed mud on either side. A short distance further on the track continued in the direction of Kings.

"He's playing with us. He may have got into Kings, but he won't get out." Clapham's tone was full of fury.

Chapter Sixty-two

The young woman driving the small Volkswagen was in a hurry to get to her office before 8 a.m. As she approached the bus stop on the edge of Kings, she was dismayed to see a policeman step onto the road in front of her signalling for her to stop. With her thoughts racing, she braked heavily and managed to stop, expecting to be cautioned about her speed.

The policeman approached the car and quickly opened the driver's door.

"Morning Miss, he said gruffly, "police emergency, I have to commandeer your car. Please step out now."

Shaking with fright and confusion, the woman grabbed her handbag and obeyed.

"You can get your car back at the station later," said the policeman as he got into the driver's seat and accelerated away.

The three people waiting at the bus stop were now very curious to know exactly what they had just witnessed.

"What the hell was all that about?" enquired one man. "Are you alright?"

"I don't know," replied the woman. "He said it was a police emergency."

"Come and sit down dear," said a woman. "You look quite shaken."

"Strange looking policeman, if you ask me," said the man. "He rode up on that old bike over there. He was wearing trainers and had an odd sweater on under his jacket. Something not right about him. I'll ask the police hot line what's going on," he said, punching some numbers into his cell phone.

The emergency call centre operator, on listening to the man's query, immediately transferred the call to the operations room, who kept the man on the line while his information was quickly passed on to Assistant Commissioner James Rossiter.

"Ask him what was the make and model of the bloody car," he yelled at the detective handling the call. Rossiter's face had reddened.

"Not only has the bastard broken the cordon, now he has hi-jacked a bloody car at a bus stop. Jesus wept," he exclaimed, "this town is cursed, and the devil is amongst us."

He put his head in his hands.

Cook knew that the alarm would soon be out. The small red Volkswagen Polo would be easily spotted, but he needed to get nearer to the Kings hall before abandoning it. He drove carefully without taking any risks. He had decided on a suitable vantage point so that he could first trigger, and then witness, his planned destruction of Kings U3A.

Chapter Sixty-three

At 8.15 Rossiter had still not moved from his position in the ops room when Clapham arrived back to report on the death of the young policeman at St Patricks. He had no sooner begun to speak to Rossiter when the supervisor of the special dog squad appeared at the door.

"Detective Clapham, I have to tell you some bad news. There was a mix-up with the dogs last week when we swept the Kings Hall. The handlers mistakenly used the drug sniffer dogs, not the dogs trained for explosives. The squad is on its way right now to carry out another sweep with the right dogs."

"Shit, how the bloody hell could anyone be that fucking incompetent?" Clapham spoke for everyone in the room. "Are you fucking telling me that there could be a bomb ticking in the hall?"

"I'm sorry sir, but mistakes will happen."

"Not when the lives of over a hundred people are on the line, you stupid bastard," yelled Rossiter, leaping to his feet. "Come on Clapham, let's move. Get to the bloody hall asap and bring your squad as well."

Within minutes three police cars, sirens blaring, were on their way to the Kings Hall. As they approached the front of the building, two dog handlers and a senior officer emerged and came down the front steps to meet them. The two beagles were frisking around their handlers, straining at their leashes.

"What's happening?" called Rossiter to the leader.

"Good news sir. We have located two packages with cell phones attached, which look like they are set up as timers. One was in the ladies' toilet, and the other under the stage. We think it's Semtex, but the army bomb squad have been on standby and will be here in a few minutes."

"Thank Christ for that. How professional do they look? The bombs, I mean."

"Pretty well standard, sir. Straight off the internet. Afghanistan, Iraq, Syria, fortunately these maniacs use the tried and true methods. They are easy to construct, which equally, makes them easy to disarm."

Twenty minutes later, at 8.50, three members of the bomb squad emerged from the hall wearing the usual heavy Kevlar reinforced clothing needed for such a dangerous task. Two were holding small packages, which they placed in non-magnetic boxes on the back of their armoured vehicle.

"All done sir," declared the senior member. "Nasty stuff, this Semtex. It has Russian markings, so the maniac who placed them must have been on tour. We will detonate them on the range. Should be fun," he added in a casual manner, having just averted a major national tragedy.

"Well done," said Rossiter, "so the meeting of U3A can proceed?"

"I don't see why not," said the man, "but it doesn't solve the problem of catching the killer, does it? I hope to God that he doesn't have a plan B."

****

"Mrs O," said Tommy, glancing across at his passenger, "there's bound to be a crowd trying to park around the hall this morning. Everyone will want to hear what our speaker has to say about stroke research. I think I'll leave the car on the other side of the park, and we can walk past the gardens to the hall."

"That's a lovely idea Tommy, the gardens are always worth a look. Let's do that."

They were on one of several paths which criss-crossed the area when Tommy noticed a man sitting on a park bench, reading a newspaper. What drew his attention was that the man was holding the newspaper upside down. He looked again, and the nightmare experience he had endured months before in the Collectibles shop flashed before him. He was looking at Sam

Cook. The short dyed hair, cap and scarf were not enough to deter him.

Motioning with his hand to his companion, Tommy whispered, "Stay back, Mrs O."

He drew the Glock from inside his jacket and quietly approached Cook.

"Hello Cook, it is you, isn't it?" he said, levelling the pistol.

Cook leapt up, raising his left hand to attack Tommy. There was a sharp crack, and Cook cried out, holding his left hand. The bullet from the Glock had passed through the base of his thumb.

"You bastard, Tomlinson," he shrilled, "now look what you have done. I should have killed you in Tallinn, but you are too late." He took out a cell phone with his right hand, blood pulsing from his wounded left hand. With his system completely in the euphoric phase of the drug which had captured his life, Cook was feeling no pain.

"This will bring down the bloody lot of them, even if the hall still isn't full," he said in a voice full of defiance.

As he began to try to punch in numbers with his right thumb, Tommy shot him in the upper chest. The force flung Cook backwards as the cell phone dropped away.

Standing over him, Tommy was ready to fire again, but there was no need.

Cook, spread-eagled on his back, his eyes still blazing red with hatred, muttered his last words.

Tommy later recalled that it sounded like a question.

"Is that you, Amelia?"

The End

Acknowledgements

When I was encouraged to join the local chapter of U3A, I had very little idea of the wonderful service that the organisation provides to oldies of all hues in many countries.

Along with its wide-ranging opportunities for learning in later life, it also provides a solid social network for many people who through age, and circumstance, would otherwise be facing a possibly lonely life with little opportunity for interaction with others of a similar age.

This is particularly so in the case of older women, who may find themselves widowed, and cut-off from former friendships attached to their late partners. In most U3A groups of my experience women outnumber men 3-1.

Voluntary community service in U3A provides an outlet for the wealth of experience in all walks of life that is present in the membership. As we say, 'everyone used to be someone'.

My life would have been very different if I had not been fortunate enough to be a member of U3A for twelve years, and counting.

www.ingramcontent.com/pod-product-compliance
Lightning Source LLC
Chambersburg PA
CBHW030448250626
47154CB00003BA/1182